OVERWIN P9-DGX-623

Ratika Kapur worked in publishing and multimedia before cutting loose to write full-time. She lives in New Delhi with her husband and son.

Praise for *Overwinter*

'*Overwinter* is a startlingly accomplished first novel, a stunning debut. Ratika Kapur ventures bravely into terrain where seasoned writers fear to tread, adeptly handling the nuances of incestuous love with sure and nimble prose.' – *Outlook*

'*Overwinter* is […] a finely-crafted novel and it's not surprising that Kapur was on the longlist for the Man Asian Literary Prize for this book.' – *Sunday Guardian*

'It is a very well-written story that makes the plot very believable. All the characters seem to jump out of the book and come alive as if it were unfolding before you.' – *Tribune*

'You are impelled to explore and think about your own relationships once you read *Overwinter*.' – *Sunday Indian*

'Foremost amongst Ratika's strengths is her use of language, lyrical and at times brutal, guaranteed to shake the reader from her sense of complacency.' – *Deccan Herald*

Overwinter

RATIKA KAPUR

First published in 2011 by Hachette India
(Registered name: Hachette Book Publishing India Pvt. Ltd)
An Hachette UK company
www.hachetteindia.com

This edition published in 2016

1

ISBN 978-93-5195-103-2

Hachette Book Publishing India Pvt. Ltd
4th & 5th Floors, Corporate Centre
Plot No. 94, Sector 44,
Gurgaon 122003, India

Typeset in Adobe Garamond Pro 11/14.5
by InoSoft Systems Noida

Printed and bound in India by Manipal Technologies Ltd, Manipal

To my wingman, Amitabha Bagchi

Summer

1

Peeling the sheet off his feet, she traces her forefinger around his toes, unready to touch them. It feels too bright. She switches off the bedside light.

His body lies quiet and motionless. She quietens her own and lies next to him. In the comfort of this new darkness, she props herself on her elbow and brings her face to his: his lips feel like a sun-dried prune. Sitting up now, she strokes his sable-soft eyebrows – black and white and thick, but tidy. Her tongue slips into his ear, lingering in its woolly bitterness. She lies down again in static cling, facing him. Her fingers toy with his Adam's apple, travel slowly under the cotton gown to the gentle pricking of his chest hair, to the rise and fall of his breathing, then to his navel; and around it her fingers go, over and over, until they move down to his cock. She flinches on first touch, her hand trembles, but on raising his gown she is stilled by the sight: an ageing calla lily; flaccid, sad, but not without beauty.

Outside, the low night sky is scumbled in olive, a blend of the grey of four a.m. and the varying yellows of the streetlights. The trees in the garden look like the amateur ink renderings she used to do. She wraps an arm and a leg around him, and closes her eyes.

Before long she is in the borderland of half-consciousness that heralds sleep; that no-zone where fantastic thoughts, pictures – a flycatcher on wheels, bleeding gingerbread men, a black cat pissing on a Steinlen poster – roll in. Then there is a sound, a sound too soft to decipher, and she is awake again. She is awake to a wall-to-wall gloom, which offers not the solace of light or no light, but leaves her adrift in the predawn dimness of nowhere.

She turns onto her back again; her uncle is still unmoving, and atop her lies only his shadow, a weightless impression of him.

It is a radiant summer morning, but with the blinds down and the curtains drawn her aunt's room is blacker than a blacked-out Delhi night. She moves inaudibly towards the bed and feels around for any breathing. When she discovers life, she climbs into bed with it. Her aunt awakens.

'Keta?' Neera says hoarsely.

'Yes, Masi.'

Clearing her throat, Neera turns over onto her side, away from her niece.

'Did you sleep all right?' Ketaki asks.

Neera does not respond.

Ketaki moves closer to her aunt, and pressing her face into Neera's back, she detects that sweet, maddening scent of Dior's Poison. Even in a nightie, groomed and perfumed. 'Did you sleep okay?' she asks again.

'You've been smoking.'

'Did you sleep okay?'

'Yes. What time is it?'

'Seven… seven thirty.'

'How is he?' Neera says, switching on the lamp by her bedside.

'Who?'

4

'Your uncle. You were in his room.'

Ketaki shifts onto her back and folds her arms below her chest. 'Someone needs to look out for him,' she says.

Pulling the bedsheet up to her chin, Neera turns off the light.

'We need to pick up surgical gloves,' Ketaki says.

Her aunt is unresponsive again.

'We need to pick up the surgical gloves.'

'Allwell can deliver. They keep everything,' Neera says.

'Okay. Could we put the blinds up?'

'No.'

Through the silence that ensues, the bedroom begins to reveal itself to Ketaki in dim contours. The outline of the Burma teak dressing table – much too grand for this room, much too grand for this age – grows visible. Now she can see the murky form of the steel Godrej cupboard, standing assertively by the bathroom door.

She lies with her aunt in the quiet of a darkened, muted morning, sharing only the muffled noises of a household at work: of furniture being shifted as the floors are mopped, of the bristly sweeping of carpets, of the intermittent whistles of a pressure cooker. Neera taps her foot lightly against hers. Ketaki dozes off to this, and to the smell of detergent mixed with half-cooked dal and Poison.

She walks down the street to her own place, a rented one-bedroom flat that her uncle Deepak found for her a year ago, when she decided not to return to New York. It is a convenient arrangement; it grants her quick access to the services of her aunt and uncle's better-functioning household, while allowing her time and space away from them.

Coming through the door and into the living room she realizes that she had left all the lights on. In fact, every electrical switch in the flat is in force. From above, the fan disperses the squawk of the news presenter on the television, Prokofiev's *Lieutenant Kijé* playing on loop on her laptop, and the air conditioner's frantic blasts. She walks through the cool illuminated noise to the sofa, melts into it, and closes her eyes.

Deepak, she thinks. Deepak Uncle, she says out loud. Suddenly she feels the need to vomit, and scrambles off the sofa and towards the bathroom. Crouching over the WC, no meal is forthcoming. Instead her stomach dry-heaves until it tires.

She returns to the sofa, pulls out a cigarette from the pack lying on the floor, strokes it from filter to tip, and lights it. Smoke uncoils around the dark shoulder-length hair that falls by the sides of her face. Setting her head down on the sofa armrest, she stretches her legs out, picks up her laptop from the coffee table next to her, and places it on her stomach. There are eighteen emails to be read. A call centre in Gurgaon would like her to design some of their marketing collateral. Would she be interested? Perhaps, but she has not stepped into the studio in over a month. Andrea, from whom Ketaki had sublet an apartment in Brooklyn, wants to visit at Christmas. A Hungarian film festival is starting next week; her cellphone bill is due; and so on. And her ex-boyfriend Lars has met someone and he thought he should tell her.

Less than twenty minutes later, Adil is sitting beside her on the sofa, holding her head to his chest as she rests against him. She messaged him; he came.

'When did the electricity go?' he says.

Although it is about thirty-eight Celsius outside, she

had not noticed when the power went. 'I don't know,' she says, peering up at the stationary ceiling fan. 'Maybe half an hour ago.'

He tries to lift her off his chest to stand up, but she presses down on him.

'Don't move,' she mumbles into his shirt pocket. 'Please.'

'I just thought I'd open a window.'

'It's okay.'

'All right,' Adil says.

'Thanks for coming.'

'Not a problem. I have no afternoon meetings.'

Trying to straighten herself, she looks up at him. He smiles and puts his arm around her.

Soothed, somehow, by the weight of him, by the heft of his arm upon her shoulders, she closes her eyes. For his part, he remains like this, like how she wants him to be: still, silent, at hand.

Her cellphone breaks the shared quiet. She lets it ring out, but when it buzzes again, she picks it up.

'I forgot about the doctor's appointment,' her aunt says quickly. 'It's at five thirty.'

'I know,' Ketaki says.

'Five thirty in the evening,' Neera says. 'Today.'

'I know.'

'Will you come?'

'Yes. I'll come by at four thirty and – '

Her aunt disconnects.

She glances at Adil, then at her phone.

'Everything all right?' he says.

'Just some work shit,' she says, slipping her phone into the front pocket of her jeans. 'A bunch of deadlines.'

'All right.'

7

She stands up and walks to the window to open it. 'It's stuffy in here,' she says, and moves across the living room towards the small round dining table.

'Come and sit,' Adil says as he tracks her movements around the table.

'Something to drink?'

'Not just now. Come and sit down.'

With slow steps she continues to circle the table. Adil goes up to her, and taking her by the hand, leads her back to the sofa.

'You're back from Sangla a little early, aren't you?' he says.

'Yes. We cut short the trip.'

'Is everything all right?'

She lights a cigarette, then reclines on the sofa with her head on Adil's lap. Gazing up at him directly, she tries to smile.

He lowers his face to kiss her on the nose.

'We saw some amazing birds,' she says, 'my uncle and I.'

'Good.'

'Redstarts. Finches. Dippers.'

'So why did you come back early?'

She turns on to her side and reaches for her laptop. Adil immediately takes it from her.

'What?' she says. 'I want to show you the birds.'

'Later,' he says. 'First tell me what's wrong.'

'Nothing's really wrong. I'm just feeling a little shitty.'

'Okay. Why?'

'I don't know. It's just one of those days, you know.'

'No, I don't know.'

'Anyway, forget about it,' she says, sitting up.

'No,' he says.

'Come on.'

'No,' he says again, this time with a degree of force.

She gets up and moves a few paces away from him. 'I have a meeting in Saket at three,' she says. 'I need to go.'

'You want me to leave.'

'Yes,' she says, now returning to his side.

After Adil leaves she returns to her laptop and pulls up Lars's email. It has been over two years since they broke up. She is happy that he has met someone and would like to tell him so. Should she also mention Deepak Uncle? Dying Deepak Uncle? But to what purpose now?

The elevator doors draw open and the two women step out. Neera looks to her left and right, and walks down the corridor that stretches out before her, with Ketaki close at heel. Scanning the doorplates on both sides, she stops outside Dr Nath's office. A nurse tells her to wait. She sits on a bench upholstered in bile-green vinyl. Ketaki sits down beside her.

A man drooped on an identical bench across from them is crying. A boy of thirteen, maybe fourteen – he has that pubescent sheen on his nose – leans on the man's right shoulder. A girl several years younger than the boy is seated to the man's left. She is sucking her thumb.

Ketaki slips off her sandals and pushes them under the bench. Resting her feet on the cool grey tiles of the hospital's third floor, she watches the man in front of her as he weeps. He cries quietly for the most part, but every now and then disgorges a sob that rushes down the corridor, splintering the even hum around them. The boy and girl look up at him, and frequently at Neera, who has picked up an old magazine from a pile on the table next to her and concealed herself behind a news story on the Indian cricket team's tour of South Africa earlier in the year.

The man opposite is weeping and he does not try to control it. He does not try to hide it. Ketaki watches the tears course down his face free from fear or shame; free from pain, perhaps. Neera puts aside the magazine. As she shuffles inside her bag, her silver pillbox tumbles out and opens onto the floor. The little girl jumps up. Thumb still in her mouth, she uses her free hand to pick up bits of clove and cardamom that have spilled out. She puts some of it into her own pocket and the rest into Neera's outstretched hand.

Looking at Ketaki – for comfort? for impetus?– her aunt gets up and flattens the pleats of her deep blue sari with her hands. The boy on the bench giggles. Neera looks away.

'Papa,' the boy says, still giggling.

Papa has leaned back. With his head resting against the wall he appears to be studying the streak of white light that runs above them.

'Papa,' the boy says again.

The man straightens up and looks at Neera. His eyes have an inflated pinkness about them. He looks at her for several moments before she turns and walks rapidly in the direction of the elevator.

'Wait,' Ketaki says. She gets up and hurries after her aunt.

Neera does not stop. She has reached the elevator lobby.

'Masi, wait,' Ketaki calls out again.

The elevator arrives. Neera steps in and it closes its doors behind her.

Ketaki continues to wait outside the doctor's office. She is fairly certain her aunt will return. Neera will walk around the Grand Central-like waiting area, baulk at the filth, loiter outside the chemist, and then she will come back.

The weeping man remains weeping and the children continue to fidget. Where is the woman among them? Where is the wife, the mother, that special presence that could quieten them all with a single gesture?

'Mrs Sood?' The nurse calls their turn.

Ketaki walks up to the nurses' station. 'Mrs Sood is in the bathroom,' she says. 'I'll just get her.' As she rummages in her bag for her cellphone to call her aunt, the elevator bell announces its approach and Neera reappears. Together they walk into the doctor's office.

Dr Nath sits behind a desk, which, at a depth of five feet, keeps him at a secure distance from the disease, the fears, the doubts of those who visit him. He motions the nurse to shut the door, reclines back on his chair, and rolls his neck. After an extraordinarily long stretch, he bends forward, resting his elbows on the desk. 'Mrs Sood,' he says, beaming at Neera. To Ketaki he offers only the briefest of smiles.

Neera sits bolt upright, her arms crossed against her chest.

'Mrs Sood,' he says again, 'it's a pleasure to see you. I'm glad you came.'

Neera does not react.

'How is Mr Sood?'

'He is well.'

'You know, I've been very concerned about your decision to take him home.'

'You said there is little hope. He is happier at home.'

'Yes, in such a severe case of cerebral hypoxia there isn't much hope,' says Dr Nath. 'But still, I'm not comfortable with the decision.'

'The nurses are good. They're on the job,' Ketaki adds.

'What about the PEG?' Dr Nath asks.

'Sorry?'

'The feeding tube.'

'All fine,' Ketaki says.

'Regular flushing?'

'Yes. After every feed.'

'Is he being turned over regularly? We're always concerned about pressure sores. And any abnormal breathing patterns – slow, laboured breathing?'

Neera takes over: 'As I said, he is happier at home. More comfortable. If any problem develops, we will call.' With that she stands up and signals Ketaki to follow.

It is a long and dusty journey home to the leafy colony that is Panchsheel Enclave in south Delhi. Much of the time is spent negotiating the fuming traffic at Nehru Place. Through the car window Ketaki looks up at the faces that hang above her from a Blueline bus. A little boy sucks in his lower lip and makes rabbit faces at her, but before she can devise a comeback the bus rumbles ahead, carrying with it the sleep and abjection and joy and belligerence it has picked up along its route. From her bag she takes out Salim Ali's *The Book of Indian Birds,* which, despite its considerable heft, she carries everywhere like a prayer book. (A second copy has been at her bedside for over a year and a half now – her most sustainable nighttime companion yet.) She had spotted a lone accipiter near the hospital that she cannot name. It was not the common Shikra lurking on high in the trees, but a bird that was darker, heartsick, more beautiful. As she turns the pages of her book trying to identify the creature, the driver, Om Prakash, bursts into a low moan without warning. Ketaki looks at her aunt, whose attention is riveted on the vehicle in front of them. The moaning grows into an incantatory wail that leaps about the car.

'How could this happen to Deepak Sahib? How? And

him? Why him?' Om Prakash heaves. 'And so young? Just like my brother, my own brother. Oh god,' he says, looking up at the roof of this new and magnificent Japanese import, suddenly noticing a lubricant stain that he immediately spits at and begins to rub clean lest Madam chances upon it. 'Oh god,' he starts again, 'you should have taken me away first. Why him? Why Deepak Sahib?' – and, magically, tears begin to pelt down his face. He is now pounding the steering wheel with the fist of his left hand, outmanoeuvring the surrounding cars with his right.

Neera and Ketaki sit behind watching the productions within and without unfold. Ketaki is about to give this broken man a pat on his shoulder, but quickly retracts. She realizes that if she wishes to indulge him, she should avoid the tepid gestures to which she is accustomed and let the driver's lamentation run unstaunched. Over here, pain that is left alone, unconsoled, makes a man – a mighty martyr – out of anyone.

'Temple,' Om Prakash says, 'we must go to the temple.' He searches for consent through the rear-view mirror, a contraption he uses for the sole purpose of communicating with backseat passengers.

Neera is outside the guest bedroom – Deepak's new quarters – with Ketaki at her side again. She grips the doorknob, her knuckles growing pale with the exercise. This is her first visit to her husband since they brought him home three days earlier. Gopal Singh, long-standing factotum at the Sood household, stands behind, galvanizing her. He says nothing, but there is persuasion in his nearness.

Neera turns the knob, opens the door, and stops. She looks to her right at the new medical bed, which has replaced the double bed. A table with a lopsided lamp sits to one side of it; the tea trolley from the dining room is placed by the other. In front of her are the small sofa-set and the aspirant coffee table that have been repositioned under the large grilled window through which the gulmohar tree pushes its way in.

After examining the room Neera comes through the doorway and inches towards the bed. 'He looks quite good,' she says to Ketaki.

The scene is almost certainly less tragic than her aunt could have imagined. Except for the single tube vanishing into his stomach, Neera's husband glows like a lady newly renewed at Mrs Petal Chopra's Spa. Deepak's hands are arranged elegantly on his stomach, fingers carefully interlocked. His face has been massaged to a soft shine, his hair is parted with precision and combed neatly to each side. This is how they try to fashion dignity in a vegetable.

'He looks quite good,' she says again. Then, as if she were fearful that this might change, that on further study her husband might betray the suffering she had expected him to display, Neera retreats from the bed and joins Ketaki on the sofa. 'I didn't order the surgical gloves,' she says.

'They should be here in half an hour,' Ketaki says. 'I called for them in the morning.'

'All right. Where is the sister?'

'I've told her she can sit in the study when we're with him.'

'But she should be here. What has one paid her for?'

'It's okay, Masi. She needs a break too.'

Neera is quiet now, quiet and restless. Perhaps she had rehearsed for another show and now does not know what to do. She gets up, attempts to straighten the bedside lamp, walks across to the bathroom door, turns around, and comes back to the sofa. She pauses, then starts to pace up and down between the bathroom at one end of the room and the window at the other, casting frequent, unfinished looks at her husband. 'We should have dinner now,' she says. 'It'll get late for Thomas.'

'It's only seven forty-five,' Ketaki says.

Neera turns to Gopal Singh. 'Bring the chair here,' she says, pointing at the bed.

He lifts the single-seater near the window and sets it down by Deepak's side.

'No, here,' she says, tapping the end of the bed.

He drags it towards the bottom of the bed and steps back.

Neera sits down. 'Thank you,' she says.

'We need to give Deepak Uncle the prasad,' Ketaki says.

'Pardon?'

'The prasad from the temple. We promised OP.'

'What about it?' Neera says.

'We need to give him some,' Ketaki says. She looks to Gopal Singh, who sits on his haunches by the window, for her next move. His short nod speaks to her, and she picks up the polythene bag that carries Baba's blessings and moves towards the inaction.

Deepak's eyes come open.

Ketaki takes a step back. 'Masi,' she says.

'Don't be ridiculous,' Neera says. 'We can't give him anything.'

'No, his eyes. His eyes are open.'

Gripping the arm of her chair, Neera slowly rises.

Deepak presents them with a pair of eyes proclaiming life in a body that has otherwise shut itself to it.

Ketaki brings her hand to his face and lightly runs her fingers up his left cheek.

Neera cannot touch her husband, so she tries to talk to him: 'Deep?' she whispers. 'Deepak?'

Deepak is quiet.

'I think we should give him the prasad,' Ketaki says. 'We could, through the gast – gastotomy tube,' Ketaki says.

'Gastrostomy tube,' her aunt says.

'Yes. We could through the – the tube. Or just put a bit up a nostril.'

'What?'

'Well, he breathes, doesn't he? He could just breathe it in.'

'Ask the sister.'

The nurse is summoned and she flounces in with toe-curling alacrity. 'Yes, what is it my dears?' Sister Shiny asks.

'We'd like to give him a bit of this prasad,' Ketaki says.

'Prasad-shasad,' Sister Shiny says, shaking her small round head at the heathen others. 'You think it will make him better?'

'We would like to give him some,' Ketaki says.

'So what is the matter then?' Shiny says. 'Give it to him. Put it in his mouth then.'

No one moves.

'Oh ho, you all are scared. Now what should we do then? It is not my religion, you know, but I will do it because it is my duty.'

'Forget it,' Ketaki says, stepping forward. 'I'll do it.'

'No, no,' the nurse says, pushing Ketaki aside. 'I will, I will. You can't.'

'I said I will do it,' Ketaki says.

Sister Shiny looks at Neera and Gopal Singh for support, but none is tendered. She about-turns and leaves the room.

Ketaki takes a pinch of the prasad with her right hand. Carefully pushing Deepak's mouth open, she sprinkles the offering on his tongue. Before her fingers are able to leave him, Deepak's lips shut around her thumb and forefinger. Gopal Singh squats by the window, too far from the moment, and Neera winces from behind her. Ketaki will prize that instant forever.

2

Her aunt is tidying up the drawing room after a Scrabble session when Ketaki comes in. Neera is wearing a pale pistachio-green handloom sari and a string of pearls, and her bobbed grey hair shimmers silver as it catches the sun through the window. In the luminosity of the noonday sun, she looks so much like Ketaki's mother Uma, only that she is heavier, older, and alive.

'Nice sari, Masi. I haven't seen it before.'

'It's forty years old.'

Ketaki sits down on the wing chair. 'Nice colour,' she says.

'Ma gave me this one. Of course, your mother got the baby pink one.'

Of course, Ketaki thinks. 'How did it go today?' she says.

'Prem Malhotra was late by half an hour,' her aunt says. 'I really think she should be thrown out of the group.' She picks up a cushion, fluffs it up, and places it on the sofa so that it sits precariously on one of its corners in the shape of a diamond, rather than be allowed to rest comfortably, squarely, on one of its sides. 'And Sheila Seth – she just cannot mind her own business. Constantly, constantly, asking about your uncle.'

Also your husband, Ketaki would like to say.

'And I played terribly. I should give it up. In any case, four times a week is too much.'

'But you enjoy Scrabble.'

'No, not any more,' Neera says. 'Actually, maybe I never really have.'

Ketaki gets up and walks towards the door.

'Lunch is ready. We're just waiting for Prakash Bhapa.'

'Prakash Mama?' Ketaki says.

'Yes. He should be here in the next fifteen-twenty minutes.'

'I'm off – I'm not really hungry.'

'He's coming especially to see you.'

As soon as the clock strikes one, the doorbell sounds and Lieutenant-General Prakash Chand Mehra (Retd), Neera and Uma's only brother, appears in the drawing room in a batik shirt and perfectly creased black trousers. Arms open in a ready embrace, he walks up to Neera and hugs her, then takes Ketaki in his hold and kisses her on her forehead.

'Good. You're both looking good,' he says, nodding and smiling at the two of them.

'Thank you,' Neera says. 'How are you, Bhapa?'

'Ah well, could be better, could be worse.'

'Are you ready for lunch?'

'Oh yes, I'm famished. I played a full eighteen holes this morning.'

Neera leads the party to the dining room and positions herself at the head of the table. She directs Prakash to sit to her left, in what was her husband's chair just a month earlier, and Ketaki sets herself down to her aunt's right.

'Now tell me, how is Deepak?' Prakash says.

'He's comfortable,' Neera says.

'Good. That's very good.'

Neera pulls her chair in a little. 'Yes,' she says. 'Some ghee on your roti?'

'No, no thank you,' he says.

'Your plate's almost empty,' she says, turning to Ketaki.

'I'm not very hungry.'

'Keta dear,' Prakash says, 'you must eat properly. I know you must be helping your masi a lot. You need the nourishment.'

'I will, a little later,' Ketaki says. 'But tell us how you're doing.'

'Oh, you won't believe it – I have over five lakh hits now! Can you believe it?'

Here it comes, she thinks, the YouTube update. On retiring from the army, her uncle Prakash decided to pursue his greatest passion of all: singing; singing old Hindi film songs. When he could not make the grade on Sahara Filmy's reality show *Bathroom Singers*, his neighbour suggested he share his hidden talents with a wider audience: the seventy-five or so million YouTube users. He has not looked back since. 'Unbelievable,' Ketaki says.

Neera smiles.

'Five lakh hits now! And once I upload the new Rafi songs I've sung, I'm sure I'll be in the top ten. I've seen the rubbish on the YouTube. Ketaki, you must know about that "Bus Uncle" video, or that Korean boy playing Pachelbel's "Canon" – it's rubbish, total rubbish. I mean, Neera, you can't believe what people watch. A video of two men having a silly altercation on a bus. So what? But god knows how many crore hits it gets. And, my god, that Korean boy… that Korean boy playing such a masterpiece on an electric guitar! Ghastly. I have to say, just ghastly. You tell your masi, Keta.'

'Ghastly,' Ketaki says. 'How's Usha Mami?'

'Fine, fine. She's at the club playing Bridge. She'll be here after lunch.'

Other than the occasional request for replenishment, the rest of the main course is eaten in silence. Neera finishes first. She plays with her napkin ring, sliding it up and down her thumb. Now she picks up her fork and taps it lightly against the rice bowl. She remains at the table, though it is clearly an effort of will.

Ketaki tries to hurry, but every morsel that goes in takes doubly long to go down. This, too, an effort of will.

'Rasgulla, Prakash Bhapa?' Neera asks, once her brother is ready for dessert.

'Only if you all are going to have one.'

Neera rings the little silver bell that is positioned next to her silver glass of water, and Thomas the cook brings forth a large bowl of rasgullas bobbing in sugar syrup. She serves Prakash.

'Ketaki, what about you?' Prakash says.

'Maybe later, thanks.'

'Neera?' he says.

'No, no thank you.'

'Doctor's orders?'

Neera picks her napkin off her lap. Slowly ironing each crease with her forefinger, she folds it.

'Wah! Outstanding!' Prakash says after his first spoonful. 'Evergreen Sweets?'

'No, they're from CR Park.'

'Ah, of course. I tell you, these Bengalis. Forget Tagore and Ray, their greatest contribution to the nation is sweets. What do you think, Keta?'

'Absolutely,' Ketaki says.

Prakash lets out a large sigh as he finishes. 'I think I'm going to need some saunf now,' he says.

Neera gestures Ketaki to fetch the small silver-filigreed chest from the china cabinet. It is set down in front of Prakash. Ketaki then stands behind him, wrapping her arms around his warm neck.

'Let us see now,' he says, pinching his chin as he surveys the range of seeds and lumps that promise to aid digestion. With the ridiculously small spoon assigned to serve them, he carefully helps himself to a blend of dry-roasted aniseed and betel nut.

Neera rings the bell again and Thomas comes in to clear the table.

'What a meal, Neera. As always, a perfect table. I have to say Keta, your Neera Masi runs her house perfectly. Like clockwork. She should have been in the army! But with such elegance. You should learn from her. Your mummy too — she was a great householder.'

Ketaki smiles at the reference to her dead mother Uma. Most mentions of her, rare as they are, have a mythical quality about them. 'Well, I've got to go now,' she says, and plants a kiss on her uncle's baldpate.

'Are you going home?' Prakash says.

'Yes, I've got a lot of work to do.'

'Actually, Usha Mami wanted to give you some brownies she picked up yesterday from Pudding and Pie. Could we drop by at your flat for a few minutes when she comes?'

'Sure,' she says.

'Will you be home for dinner?' Neera asks.

'Probably not,' Ketaki says, coming around the table to kiss her aunt goodbye. 'I'll call you.'

•

The doorbell rings. The Mehras have arrived at her flat with big smiles and a box of brownies. She steers them into the living room.

'Keta,' Prakash says, once several rounds of tea and brownies have been had, 'we know that Deepak Uncle is very unwell and that this may not be the right time, but some things cannot wait. Usha Mami and I need to talk to you about something.'

'Okay,' she says, correcting her posture.

'Well, I don't know if you remember my friend Vijay Nanda. We've been golfing partners for many, many years.'

'No, I'm sorry I don't.'

'Well, he has a son, Siddharth, a very fine young man, who has just returned from America.'

'You're right,' she says, 'it probably is the wrong time to bring this up.'

'Keta dear,' Usha says in her softest tone, 'things like marriage can't be delayed. We know how close you are to Deepak Uncle. This is a very difficult time for you. But you know, you're almost twenty-nine. You're not getting any younger, and there aren't many eligible boys left.'

'Mami, please,' she says. 'I'm okay this way.'

'Dear, do it for Deepak Uncle. It would make him so happy.'

Would it? Ketaki wonders.

'And Siddharth really is a very fine young man,' Prakash adds. 'He has an MBA from Stanford University. Stanford University, Keta – better than Ivy League! A very, very intelligent young man. Mummy?' he says, turning to his wife.

'Yes. Your uncle is absolutely right,' Usha says, taking her husband's cue. 'And mind you, it was his own decision to move back to India. You know, his mother was saying that so many companies here were wooing him to join them. I tell you, one day lunch at the Oberois, one day dinner at Imperial... He is finally going to join some small fancy personal equity – '

'Private equity, Mummy,' Prakash interjects.

'Yes, private equity, a private equity boutique type of company – boutique.'

Ketaki smiles.

'And his parents are such fine people,' Prakash says. 'We've known them for almost forty years.'

'Yes, a very fine couple. One thing, dear,' Usha says, placing her hand on Ketaki's thigh, 'Mrs Nanda – Shireen – is Muslim. But, I tell you, she's very modern, very broadminded – just like us.'

'Yes, yes, she's very open-minded, Keta,' Prakash says. 'You don't have to worry.'

Ketaki picks up another brownie and nibbles at it.

'See, dear, there's no harm in meeting him,' Usha says. 'And we're only asking you to meet him. Nothing else. No pressure. We oldies will not interfere. No, Daddy?'

'No, no, we will not interfere. Keta, we were also young once. We also did things like dating and necking. Before I met your aunty, I knew this English girl, Margaret, and we had coffee and – '

'You both meet on your own,' Usha breaks in. 'If you both hit it off, fine, and if you both don't like each other, that's also fine.'

'Margaret was a highly qualified nurse in England,' Prakash continues. 'She worked at the very prestigious St George's Hospital.'

'Highly qualified?' Usha says. 'She gave Marlon Brando an enema. That's all she could boast about.'

'Mummy,' Prakash says.

'Isn't that true?' she says. 'Anyway, forget all that. Keta, there is really no harm in just meeting him.'

'Okay, I'll think about it,' Ketaki says.

'Of course, you must think,' Usha says. 'Thinking is good.'

'Thank you,' Ketaki says, standing up.

'Anyway, we should take your leave now. Mummy?' Prakash takes Usha by the hand and helps her up.

'You just think and let us know, dear,' Usha says, as she rises. 'But I have no doubt you both will hit it off like a house on fire.'

After spending three days unread in her inbox, she clicks on her father's email. Vikram Khanna is concerned. From far away and on high in a penthouse on New York's Upper East Side, he is concerned about the situation in New Delhi: he is concerned about how his daughter and his sister-in-law Neera are coping with Deepak's condition; he is concerned about whether Ketaki has called Krishan to have the leaks in the roof of her apartment checked before the monsoon arrives; he is concerned about why she has not deposited the cheque he sent to her. Vikram's email also lists all that she has missed out on by not visiting him this summer – tea-smoked duckling at Bouley and Shakespeare in the Park and weekends in Montauk – before it closes with love, with love from him and his partner Megan.

The cheque her father had FedExed to her sits on the coffee table in front of her. It came in three weeks ago, but she has yet to muster the charm required to pull a government bank teller away from his tea talk so that he can deposit a dollar cheque. For that matter, she has not even had the batteries for the power inverter changed. The tasks in themselves are not difficult to perform, it is the various people she must become in executing them: the sexy but helpless girl coyly pleading with the bank uncle to deposit her cheque; the hard-as-nails householder who will not be ripped off by a wily electrician. And sometimes these versions of her seem more real than her real self.

Her hands are poised over the keyboard for a moment before they collapse to her sides. She closes her laptop, then opens it again, bangs out a quick email to Vikram of almost true but entirely fitting responses – just the sort of reply that would warm the cockles of her father's heart – and falls asleep.

Several hours later the doorbell rings. She awakens, and walking towards the door she discovers that it has grown dark outside.

'Madam is calling you,' Gopal Singh says.

'What time is it?'

'Almost eleven.'

'Eleven? What happened?'

Gopal Singh does not answer. His gravitas offers no clues. This is typical of him. He wears his solemnity with pride and uses it effectively to discourage social exchange.

'Tell your madam it's the middle of the night.'

'Come,' he says. 'Madam is waiting.'

She shuts the door and goes into her bedroom. Madam, she thinks, as she slips on her sandals.

'Quickly, Baby,' Gopal Singh says, as they walk up the street to her aunt's. 'Madam is waiting.'

Gopal Singh leads her to the verandah, to where her aunt stands waiting. As soon as Neera sees Ketaki, she turns around and moves towards the dining room. Ketaki follows, still carrying the scent of sleep. Neera pulls out a chair from

26

under the dining table and sits down. Ketaki switches on the pendant light and sits opposite her.

Neera sits stiff and straight, almost bellicose. Her eyes allow very little in and nothing out. So Ketaki sits quietly, looking at her aunt every now and then, otherwise outlining the kalamkari pattern on the tablecloth with her finger.

'You didn't come for dinner,' Neera says. 'You didn't even call.'

'I fell asleep.'

'Gopal Singh will heat up some food for you.'

'I'm not hungry.'

Neera's head, just slightly tilted to the left, looks a little too heavy for her neck to support, but she is still combative. 'You didn't even finish your lunch,' she says.

'I'm not hungry, thank you.'

'As you wish.'

'How is Deepak Uncle?'

'Ice cream?' Neera asks.

Ice cream? Ketaki thinks. It is almost fucking midnight. Tell me what you really want. 'I'm not hungry,' she says, and puts her head down on the table.

'The night nurse actually came today,' Neera says, pushing her chair back.

Ketaki looks up at her aunt. 'That's good,' she says. 'Would you like me to stay?'

'But the day nurse is a little so-so. Smells of coconut oil.'

'Would you like me to stay?' Ketaki asks again.

'It's late.' Neera stands up.

Ketaki follows her aunt into the bedroom. Pulling out a pillow from under the bedspread, she lies down on the bed. As a child she spent night after night right here in this bed, right here between Deepak and Neera, in the warm assurance of two warm bodies. 'Really, I can stay if you like.'

'If I like?' Neera calls out from the bathroom.

'Yes,' Ketaki says, pressing her nose into the pillow, hoping for some residual whiff of her uncle.

'Do you really want to stay here for me?'

Ketaki lifts her face up from the pillow. 'What do you mean?' she says.

'Never mind,' her aunt says. 'Anyway, you better go now.'

Her first thought upon returning to the flat is to call Krishan, but on slightly deeper reflection she realizes that it is not what is in her pants that requires attention as much as other intimate spaces. Tactical substitution must begin immediately, and Krishan is hardly a replacement for Deepak.

She fills up a bucket of water to bathe and undresses as the water runs.

The specifics are a little unclear, she thinks, as she steps into the bath area. She is unable to pinpoint what exactly it is that is no longer in her life and demands substitution. Other than a man named Deepak Sood, which means nothing at all. You cannot simply replace one person with another. You do not go hunting for that one special person who will take the place of the one who has gone; instead you determine what that man (or woman) who died or disappeared did for you and find three or five or ten people who can play some of his roles, act some of his parts – books, work, birdwatching, those sorts of things help, but only marginally.

Still wet, she comes out and stands in front of the mirror in her bedroom, waiting for the hot air circulating from the fan above to dry her body. The only time she thinks she looks beautiful is now, at night, after her bedtime bath. She is beautiful, then, only for herself, and that is all right.

She opens the cupboard, takes out a T-shirt, and surprise, it is one bought by Deepak, when they went for the French Open in 2005. This is precisely the reason why it cuts so deep. A person whom you allow to love you touches not just you, but everything around you – like a contagion; like a contagion that infects T-shirts and chairs and rabbit wine-openers.

She goes out to the terrace. The sky is clear and the stars are out, though dim in their shining, perceptible only to those who seek them out. Across the street, topless Mr Chatterji is sitting on a cane chair on his terrace clipping his toenails under the light of the streetlamp. She steps back and lies down on the charpoy set in the middle of the terrace.

So the point is not Deepak's person, she thinks, but Deepak's functions that need to be substituted. The issue at hand is to identify what it was that he provided and which she now misses, so that she can seek appropriate alternatives. Sex can be ruled out – it was not really a language they spoke. There might have been the long embrace they shared from time to time, especially when he visited her in Brooklyn, or the occasional grabble, but they made no love – they never even quite kissed. Mostly the two of them would just lie close and tight, and they would sleep that special sleep that only comes in the nearness of someone you love.

But he gave her time. What is more precious a gift than that? After her mother died, who tutored her before her Hindi exams? Who would accompany her to her tennis lessons in the scorching summer sun? Who told her stories about her mother? Who sat patiently beside her while she birdwatched? Her father may have funded her childhood, her aunt may have supervised it, but Deepak gave her time. And what about her career in design? Although Uma Khanna née Mehra was one of India's finest book illustrators, she even did a little painting on the side, Ketaki was too young to engage in any significant way with her mother's work. Again it was Deepak who encouraged her to paint and draw, who helped her make a life of it.

No, she thinks, turning on her side, Deepak gave her everything, and trying to inventory all that he gave and all that he did is a futile exercise. It is what it is. No single person can provide her with everything she wants like he did. So she will divide herself, compartmentalize her needs. This would be the only way to manage the absence. It would also be a safer and more efficient method of self-governance.

Her cellphone beeps. It is a text message from Adil checking on how she is feeling. She sits up on the charpoy and considers whether he might be the man for her current mood. Adil. Adil, whom she first met at the Gymkhana Club bar about six months after her return to India. It was a Thursday, she remembers, Special Dependants' Night, when children of well-heeled Delhiites can sign for drinks and food without depending on their member mummy-papas, though they are often there themselves. She had come with one such dependant – or Green-card Holder, as the club calls them – her old school friend Priya. Amid those patrons shouting to the abdars for more masala peanuts and Scotch and beer, and those attempting to make easy preprandial conversation, amid all that and the band playing 'Volaré', Adil Merchant was pointed out to her.

I have to introduce you to this guy, ya, Priya had said, putting her arm around Ketaki. I can't tell you, he's a damn sweet guy. A totally sweet guy – really. And I know you guys would like get along really well. Adil was sitting on a stool at the bar. Dressed in a chocolate-brown shirt and blue jeans, he was making engaged and animated conversation with an elderly couple. He had a pleasing, square-cut face and looked like he was in his late thirties – his wavy tousled hair was lightly flecked with grey. And, yes, he looked like a sweet guy. Really.

Now listen, ya, Priya went on, he's like one of India's most successful corporate lawyers. Pepsi? Client. Nike? Client. Nokia? You know, he's got like every big MNC as his client. Rahul says he's damn powerful. Achha, but one thing I must tell you, she said, gripping Ketaki's forearm: He's divorced, ya – sorry. But you know, he pays like two point five lakhs a month in alimony. He fully takes care of her. And she's the one who left him. Poor guy, ya. It's really sad – really. Uff, Priya then said, and she promptly got up and wove her way towards Adil.

Ketaki, meanwhile, could do little more than light up a cigarette and watch.

Adil was still absorbed in conversation with the couple when Priya approached him, but as soon as he saw her he stood up and hugged her. His manner demonstrated nothing of the professional success or the personal failure that Ketaki had just been told of. He simply seemed like a happy, well-adjusted person; a happy, well-adjusted, and unremarkable person. They now turned to look at Ketaki and collectively smiled at her, and as she smiled back – what else could she do? – they walked in her direction.

Adil Merchant then called five days later, asking her for dinner in a half-Oxbridge, half-Parsi inflection, and the following Saturday she found herself at a sprawling home set amidst a farm in Kapashera, off the Delhi–Jaipur highway, sipping some fancy Pinot Grigio with him and his mother.

She had been wrong about Adil, and was glad to be proven so. He is a fairly happy person, but not painfully happy, and well adjusted only insofar as he is a responsible and functioning member of society. As for his seeming unremarkability, that had been a gross misjudgement on her part. What she had taken to be a general lack of distinction is actually an absence of posturing.

Although they understand each other for the most part and share a lot in common, for better or worse, she and Adil have grown to be just friends. She is uncertain why it came to be like this. Is it that they both share a general distrust of intimacy? Everyone carries baggage, and at twenty-eight and thirty-seven respectively, it could be a bit of a load. Or could it simply be that they do not want to bump fuzzies with each other? Things could change, but she doubts it.

So if she were to call Adil right now, she thinks as she rises from the charpoy, he would willingly meet her, even at this hour. He would most likely send her the car and driver – he does not think women should drive alone in the dark, carless stretches surrounding his place – they would drink wine in the patio with his insomniac mother, after which Mama Merchant would excuse herself because she knows, and rightly so, that her son is safe, and once she left they would talk about anything they cared to, without much fear of judgement or reproach, as close friends do.

But talking is exactly what she does not need.

As is customary of Krishan's arrival, the doorbell rings in continual short bursts until she makes her appearance. She walks down the stairs to the main door to open it. He comes in, shakes her hand, and shuts the door. 'See, you call and I'm here,' he says. 'Where's your landlord?'

She smiles, says nothing.

Without delay he begins to undress himself, tearing off his clothes with theatrical force. Standing within cock-reach of her, he rubs himself to a stiff glow, while she smirks at the stage show. Once he is ready, she turns towards the staircase, stops, and positions herself on the first step. He growls, pushing her shoulders towards the stairs until she is lying face down, bottom up in a perfect slant, ready to be taken by the hottest roofing expert in the National Capital Region.

The mynas outside awaken her – *radio-radio-radio*. *Radio-radio-radio*, loudly, reproachfully. She would like to hurl stones at them, but she also likes how their heads bob as they make their racket. For the first time in close to three weeks she has managed five hours of uninterrupted sleep. She should have called Krishan earlier.

Twisting around in bed in the humid post-coital residue of the night before, she inhales the faint bouquet of semen and Brylcreem. It was as good as ever last night, she thinks: no kissing, no groping with good manners; just nice, hard fucking, followed by his timely departure.

Now what if she were to agree to meet this new guy Siddharth? she thinks as she disentangles herself from the bedsheet. It would entail the same set-up rigmarole again: the dull getting-to-know-each-other conversations during the first encounter, the fiddling and fondling of the next date – if, miraculously, there is a second date, and if he is bold enough to make moves on her – followed by weeks of restless questioning and frustrating quests for what makes the other warm in the heart and hot in the groin. It is not what she wants. She would rather stick with Krishan. Siddharth would also turn out to be just another member of her breed, her south and central Delhi-centric, club-going, English-speaking, Hindu Punjabi breed. Is that what she wants? She would much rather have Krishan, Krishan in whom she has found herself a wormhole that connects her to a parallel life, that allows her to take temporary flight from the one she must otherwise endure.

When she enters Deepak's room she sees Om Prakash. One other is one too many. If OP were not around she would glide to her uncle as Usas, auspicious dawn, and she would lift her dress and ride him. In her shining, this lady of light, daughter of the sky, would stir him from his slumber, as she does all living creatures, two-footed and four. Like a swift warrior she would repulse the dark, claim the dwelling that it relinquished, and raise him to consciousness. But Om Prakash, who rests on his heels by Deepak's side, comes in the way of her triumph. 'Ji, where's the nurse?' she asks.

'She's gone to have her lunch.'

'Where is Masi?'

'Madam has gone out with Prem Madam.'

She sits down on the sofa.

'But see,' Om Prakash says, pointing at Deepak, 'Sahib's eyes are open. Sahib opened his eyes. He opened his eyes and looked at me.'

She walks up to the bed, and sure enough, his eyes are open again. But do they see? The doctor had warned them. He had told them that Mr Sood's cerebral cortex, responsible for higher cognitive functioning, had been damaged in a manner that rules out any return to consciousness, and so he will never again think, reason, remember, feel; however, since the hypothalamic and brainstem function is sufficiently preserved, he will breathe on his own, he will shit and he will piss, and his heart will continue to beat. He may also open his eyes from time to time – even moan, groan, stretch, smile. But, the doctor had cautioned them, but remember, these are involuntary responses.

'See, this is because of Baba's blessings,' Om Prakash says.

Hope is a deadly salve, she thinks, but if OP is naïve enough – lucky enough? – to be soothed by it, why stop him? 'Yes,' she says.

'Baby, will you stay here till Madam comes back? My motorcycle isn't working. I need to take it to the mechanic.'

She does not trust herself. Alone with her uncle, she thinks she might jump him. 'Can you wait a little while?'

'The mechanic said he will leave the garage after lunch. Madam should be back very soon.'

'Okay,' she says. 'I'll be here with him.'

'You'll definitely be here until Madam comes back? She said she will be back by two.'

'Yes.'

'Are you sure? I promised Madam...'

'Don't worry. I'll be here.'

He stands up. 'Then I should go now,' he says.

'Yes.'

Om Prakash shakes his head as he bows before Deepak and touches his feet. 'I feel so sad. So sad,' he says, wiping his dry eyes with his sleeve. 'This family has suffered so much. First your mother, now this. I feel so sad. You know, this is like my family.' He turns to look directly at Ketaki. 'You must get married now. That is all that is left to hope for. Get married and bring the joy of children to this house.'

'Yes,' she says. She can just see how the pitter-patter of little feet will do that. 'How's your daughter Shanti?'

'She's fine, she's happy. Her children are growing up well.'

'That's good. It's been so many years since I've seen her.'

'Yes, she is at her in-laws' house.' Om Prakash says. 'She has grown up a lot. A wife and a mother now. A wife and a mother.'

'That's nice,' Ketaki says. 'Anyway, you should go and get your bike fixed.'

'Yes, I'll go now. But please, you, only you, can bring some happiness to this – '

They hear the main door shut.

'Madam has come,' Om Prakash says, and charges out to receive her.

Ketaki is about to sit by Deepak's side when her aunt enters. Neera comes up to the bed, looks at her husband, then immediately turns around to make for the door.

'Masi? Where are you going?'

'No – nowhere,' Neera says, her voice aquiver, and she disappears.

As soon as Sister Shiny springs into the room, Ketaki joins her aunt in the study.

'Have you had your lunch?' Neera asks, realigning a painting on the wall.

'No,' Ketaki says. 'Where were you?'

'Oh, Prem Malhotra insisted I go with her for an IWG meeting. My old college friend Santosh Talwar was giving a talk on the khayal form. She sang too. Awful – just awful. Her voice really needs work.'

It is Neera Sood who probably needs work, Ketaki thinks – she might be the one who needs to adjust the timbre of her mood and the tone of her thoughts.

Her aunt is now adjusting the fall of the curtains. 'I don't know why I agreed to go,' she says.

'It's the first time you've been out in over a month,'

Ketaki says, picking up the newspaper from the coffee table.

'So? One is happy to spend time on one's own.' Once the curtains have been attended to, Neera sits down. 'And I really don't like these sorts of affairs,' she says. 'All those bored, rich Indian women trying to curry favour with diplomat wives. These get-togethers are going to become like page-three parties.'

'Don't take it so seriously then. Just take it as a people-watching exercise. That can be fun.'

'His eyes were open,' Neera says, her own eyes momentarily closed.

'I know,' Ketaki says, setting the newspaper down.

'His eyes were open and I just couldn't – you know, there was so much traffic today. Even at one in the afternoon.'

'You couldn't what?'

Neera looks at Ketaki.

'Masi, you said his eyes were open,' Ketaki says. 'What couldn't you do?'

'Imagine, it's the first time in twenty-odd years that I've forgotten to wind this thing,' Neera says, looking down at her wristwatch.

'Masi, his eyes were open. What couldn't you do?'

'Have you had your lunch?'

'Yes.' Submitting to the unlikelihood of getting her aunt to talk, Ketaki picks up her keys. 'Anyway, I've got to go now,' she says.

She slips out to the garden at the back of the house where a loud party of Jungle Babblers hops about on the ground. As soon as she steps onto the grass, the birds break into a hysterical concert of screeches, then disband and fly pell-mell into the banyan tree by the boundary wall. She takes off her sandals and dials Krishan.

'So madam is missing me already...'

'Hi.'

'Hello, hello,' he says. 'How are you?'

'Fine. You need to come and fix the roof.'

'Yes, yes. See, you made me so horny last night, man, that I forgot to tell you your daddy called me seven or eight days ago. He is worried his little princess will get wet in the rain. I will come next week to check the roof. Or if you want I will come earlier.'

'No, that's fine. Next week's fine.'

'So, what are you doing?' Krishan says.

'Nothing much,' she says. 'Where are you right now?'

'Site.'

'Okay.'

'Do you want to come?' he says.

'I'm tired.'

'Why don't you come in the morning to Gurgaon? My daddy is going to Meerut. No one will be in the office.'

'Let's see. Anyway, I have to go now.'

'Me too, man. The contractor is here.'

'All right. Bye.'

'See you tomorrow.'

She lights up a cigarette, slowly walks around the garden once, quickens her pace, and walks around it again. Soon tired, she puts her sandals back on and heads home.

3

As she approaches the end of Aurobindo Marg, the traffic has slowed to footpace as those who want to turn left are mostly in the right lane and those who need to go straight are everywhere. But during this gridlock – one of many she expects – the Qutab Minar emerges above an island of neem, imli, and pilkhan trees. Against an ashen midmorning sky, the minaret stands taller and lovelier than at any other time of day.

Several minutes and near-misses later, she manages to make the required left turn towards the Mehrauli–Badarpur intersection. She is in the middle lane now with every kind of mid- and high-capacity passenger carrier on either side closing in on her; this is classic v-formation flying, only much more fun because members of the flight have flouted every rule of relative motion. She slows down again, reaches the intersection, then stops. Now she is free to view the recently constructed Crescent Mall, hotspot for haute couture. In about three minutes she has covered some nine hundred years of history.

The light changes and she pushes ahead, only to come to another halt, at a checkpoint. It is not cops who stop her; it is that four packed lanes of cars are merging into a single six-foot-wide split between the police barriers. But she looks left, like she has done on every visit to Gurgaon, to be struck by the fifty-tonne statue of Mahavir sitting in stately repose. She inches through the barriers and, suddenly, the road opens up to her. She cruises at a comfortable forty, past the neglected but doggedly beautiful greens of Delhi's only archaeological park, and promises herself to visit the tombs of Balban, Jamali, and Kamali once the weather turns.

Andheria More arrives quicker than she had thought. Weaving through a cattle slalom course she comes to the Chhattarpur crossing. She will not turn left, towards the glamorous new temple complexes and the even more glamorous farmhouses down that road, but continues on straight, through a landscape of synchronous destruction and construction – between the casualties of the MCD's demolition drive and the towering Metro work sites. Dodging potholes and call-centre Qualises and more free-range cattle, the thicket that is Arjan Garh Air Force Station rolls by, followed by the gleaming Claremont Hotel & Convention Centre and the local wrestling pit, which, sadly, has no one moshing in the mud at this time. As the Haryana border approaches the tempers of her fellow-drivers seem to run higher; their patience thins. For her, somehow, this is right. Amidst the honk and screech, the barbaric energy, there emerges an experience that is strong enough to feel.

She is as much a secret in Krishan's life as he is in hers, so they meet at his office – a bungalow illegally used for commercial purposes, like most other residential plots in the vicinity. Few words are exchanged, but that is not what they are here for. She barely manages a hello, and Krishan has stripped off his little singlet and shorts, and is now working on her clothes. They grope and fumble and thrash about around a suite of Godrej steel furniture, finally settling for the floor. With his hands clasped tight on her hips, she rides him; now hard and fast, now slowing down. Leaning back a little, she closes her eyes, but from out of nowhere Deepak and Neera drift into her vision. As Krishan sits up and nibbles on her nipples, her uncle and aunt parade before her. She opens her eyes and rides him harder. His body tenses, he groans, and he comes. She grinds on until she aches, then gets off and grabs a cigarette.

'Sorry, man,' Krishan says. 'Too fast.'

'That's okay.'

'Do you want me to eat you?'

'No, it's okay.'

'Would you like tea?'

'Yes, please.'

Still naked they sit together on a rexine sofa sipping tea.

'How's business?' she asks.

'Quite good. My daddy has imported some hi-tech machinery from Korea. Really cool equipment, man.'

'That's great.'

'It is good, it will help us a lot,' he says. 'But you won't believe what happened. It is too funny, man. When we went to pick up the machines, we had to bribe the customs officers. Guess what we did?'

'What?'

'We gave them Black Label bottles filled with tea.' Laughing, he slaps his thigh.

She smiles.

'Really, yaar. My daddy asked my mummy to make some light tea without milk and we poured it into empty Black Labels. And they happily took them – those customs officers – thinking it was imported whiskey. Too funny.'

'Very inventive.'

'Ya, man,' he says. 'How is your daddy?'

'He's well, thanks.'

'I like your daddy. You know, he is the best client I have. He always pays on time. I send him the bill and the cheque comes. No reminders. No three dozen phone calls. No trouble. And he talks with respect. Such a big man, but he always talks respectfully.'

'Yes,' she says as she watches him stroke his bare six-pack. Every so often she questions why she meets Krishan, but it is clear to her now. What they share is special because it is not bogged down by the horrors of forever. When after the monsoon last year he sat beside her on the sofa calculating an estimate for her leaky roof, then turned to her, told her she was hot, so hot and so sexy, and kissed her, she knew that this was not going to be something long and complicated. She walked into it knowing from the outset that it would not last, and such an approach, she believes, allows for a freer kind of loving – yes, loving; fuck-buddies they may be, but a feeling that resembles love does grow. The preclusion of eternity and its sundry issues leaves her to savour the sensations of the present.

'And how is your work?' Krishan says. 'Are you using the cool new drawing board I made for you?'

'I've been using it a lot,' she says. 'Work's been quite busy.'

'As Daddyji says, work is worship.'

'Yes,' she says, lighting up another a cigarette.

'You are smoking too much, man.'

'I know.'

'See, you should not. You should stop. You know, there is a hakim in Chandni Chowk who can make you stop. Daddyji went to him and now for ten years he has not smoked even one cigarette. You should go to him.'

'Maybe I should.'

'Now, yaar, I have to go to the site. The contractor will eat my head if I am late.'

Post-retirement Deepak decided that Ketaki needed a studio of her own, and he spent the better part of last winter on her terrace overseeing its construction. Once it was completed, he devoted hours and hours of his time to her work. He helped in managing her clients, maintaining the books, even trying to acquire new business.

She unlatches the door and steps into the studio. The muck and swelter of the world outside have found their way into it. Her cool new drawing board sits in the centre of the room under a fine layer of dustmeal. She draws a long line through it with her finger, then walks slowly along the shelves, which are simply planks of plywood set upon bricks and stacked floor to ceiling against the two longer walls of the room. Her uncle had suggested this so that the height of a shelf could be adjusted based on what needed to be stored – CDs, folios, books, the odd canvas. The shelves, too, are shrouded in dust. She sits down at her workstation by the window and turns on the computer. However, on seeing Deepak's handwriting on several scraps of paper pinned to the corkboard – 'CALL MIRCHI MEDIA', 'AIRTEL customer service 9810098200', 'NECK ROTATIONS!!' – she gets up and leaves.

She lied to Krishan. Forget working a lot, post-accident this is the first time she has stepped into the studio. Her brain has been brimful of ideas, especially after her April visit to the Wilanow Poster Museum in Warsaw with her father, but now those ideas lay dying like her uncle and, unlike her uncle, they are waiting to be brought back to life.

She comes back to her bedroom and sits on the edge of the bed. The hours need to be filled, she thinks, but time is no longer governed by the diktats of TAI; it does not care how long the sun takes to travel across the sky; it could not give a shit about the phases of the moon or the beat of a heart. Time now follows its own set of mysterious laws. Each second is elastic. One minute, one minute is a day, another minute it is but a picosecond. As she lies back on the bed, she can feel the blood in her body rush upwards. Slowly it collects in pools in her head. Her eyes close, and soon sleep falls upon her like a barbiturate buzz.

She wakes up acidic at close to six in the evening. Other than the cup of tea with Krishan this morning and a couple of glasses of water, she has not had anything to eat or drink all day. She makes herself some toast, and during the process decides that she and her sick head cannot be left alone tonight.

Scrolling through a fairly short list of contacts on her cellphone she settles on Priya Kapur. Adil is too close a friend now, Krishan she met this morning, and the others are as good as strangers. Priya, on the other hand, she has known long, but never intimately – and that is a good thing. They share a common set of cultural experiences – the same school, the same neighbourhood, the same club – but how they have approached these experiences is wildly divergent. This has kept them both together and apart. It also somehow ensures that their conversations are restricted only to what is happy and fashionable and scandalous in the world; there is no danger of finding themselves in an exchange that is emotionally or intellectually demanding; say, a moment of truth or an intense political debate, which right now she simply could not handle.

Priya picks up the phone on the first ring. 'KK?' she sings. 'Hi, ya. You'll live such a long life. I was just going to call you.'

'How are things?' Ketaki says.

'Good, ya. Rahul's just got back from London. Really, he's travelling too much. I've made him promise that from now on he'll take me with him on his foreign trips. Otherwise, ya, it's just too much. I told him that one day I will forget I have a husband and then he'll know.' Priya giggles. 'Achha, but forget all that. Tell me, how are you? We must meet, ya. It's been a damn long time.'

'What are you doing tonight?'

'Nothing. You want to come for dinner? Mama and Daddy will be at the club.'

'Can I come now?'

'Ya, sure. I have to get all your news. You're my only single friend, ya – the only one who has an exciting life.'

Ketaki smiles to herself. 'So I'll be there in twenty minutes,' she says.

'Great, ya. See you.'

The watchman outside Priya's house is twirling his baton like a leader in a marching band. He salutes Ketaki when he sees her, then opens the gate and lets her in. Walking through the short drive, she passes an assortment of precisely lined-up German and Japanese cars. Priya is at the main door in white capris and a sequined T-shirt, her hair fried straight down to her shoulders.

'Hey, you're looking damn good, ya,' Priya says, as she gives Ketaki a welcome hug. 'Have you lost weight?'

'Not really.'

'You're so slim as it is. Did you walk here?'

'Yes.'

'Uff-o. You should have told me. I could have easily sent you the car.'

'That's okay. I needed the walk.'

'Achha, now come inside. It's so humid, ya. I mean look at my hair.'

Although the façade of the house belongs to a flourishing fazenda in Portugal, the inside is a pastiche of Ionic columns and Carrara marble and Balinese woodwork, a testament to Priya's father-in-law Dinesh Kapur's long and successful diplomatic career with the Indian Foreign Service. As they make their way through, a little pug comes skipping down the staircase and leaps into Priya's arms.

'Have you said hello to aunty?' she gushes, kissing the dog's ear. 'Poochie, say hello to aunty.'

Ketaki makes a few feeble gestures towards the animal.

'Achha, never mind. Bad doggie,' Priya says, setting Poochie loose. 'Go tell Mohan to bring us some tea.'

They are finally seated in the informal drawing room, also called the family room, on the first floor. Mohan is buzzed for, and tea and chilli cheese toast are brought in forthwith.

'Okay, I want all your news, ya,' Priya says, twisting the dried ends of her hair around her fingers. 'I haven't seen you since god knows when.'

'Not much has been happening – it's just the usual shit,' Ketaki says, enjoying the growing ease of being in this room, of being seated on a generously stuffed damask sofa, of being with her occasionally silly, but always affectionate friend.

'Don't lie, ya. Come on. You're so boring.'

'It's taken you twenty years to figure that out?'

They laugh.

'Have you been seeing Adil?' Priya asks, her right eyebrow arched.

'Yes, just a couple of days ago.'

'And... ?'

'And what?'

'Come on, ya, don't be so boring.'

Ketaki bites into the chilli cheese toast.

'Uff. You know, KK, you're so stupid,' Priya says, giving Ketaki a playful smack on her knee. 'You guys would make such a great couple. I mean he's such a sweet guy.'

'That he is.'

'Then? Achha, if not him, then why not someone else?'

'So what have you been up to?' Ketaki says.

'I know you're just trying to change the subject,' Priya says, with another little slap on Ketaki's knee. 'But I've been really busy, ya. The shop is doing fine. I moved it to the new Saket mall. I have some orders from Dubai and Pakistan, so now I also have to spend a lot of time at the factory, which frankly, ya, is damn pissing off. Sometimes there's no electricity, sometimes there's no water. Uff. I don't even know how people can live in Faridabad. And Rahul's like, Why do you waste your time with all this shit when you don't need to? And I'm like, Whatever, I'm doing it because I want to.'

'That's good,' Ketaki says. 'And how are your parents?'

'They just came back from the States. Oh, I have to show you this Coach bag Mummy got me. It's totally cool, ya. But they're fine. They live close to the mall so I have lunch with them. I mean my in-laws are damn cool. They don't ever object to me like going to my parents' home or whatever. So it's totally cool.'

'That's good.'

'And you? How are your masi and uncle?'

'They're well, thanks.'

47

'And your dad? You know, I haven't seen him in so long, ya.'

'He's fine. He hasn't visited in a while.'

'He has a girlfriend, no? An American girlfriend?'

'Yes, but she's English.'

'You know, now that I'm a married lady I can tell you,' Priya says, her lips moving into a pout. 'Ya, I used to think your uncle was so cute when we were in school. Actually all us girls did. But then your whole family is like so good looking. Even your mother was like a movie star. We all used to be like, Wow, she's so beautiful.'

Ketaki smiles.

'But your uncle, I mean he's like totally hot.'

It is true, Ketaki thinks. Deepak was beautiful then and continues to be so as he perishes. Even so, the strong, near faultlessness of his features remain: the tear-shaped nostrils, those bowlike lips, the jawline that meets the slight but exquisite cleft of his chin. And the structure of his face, perfectly balanced, still has the bilateral symmetry that evolutionary biologists celebrate for its universal appeal.

'Earth calling KK, Earth calling KK,' Priya announces. 'Ya, are you okay?'

'I'm fine.'

'What are you thinking about? Tell me, no...?'

'My uncle is trying to set me up.'

'Deepak Uncle?'

'No, my mother's brother Prakash.'

'Cool, ya!' Priya says. 'Who's the boy?'

'I don't know. Some guy who's just moved back to India.'

'Cool, ya! What does he do?'

'I'm not sure, but he's working in something related to finance, I think.'

'Wow. What's his name? Tell me, please. I swear I won't tell anyone.'

'It doesn't matter if you do,' Ketaki says. 'It's Siddharth. Siddharth Nanda.'

'Damn. I don't know him. Maybe Rahul will,' Priya says. 'So when are you going to meet him?'

'I'm not.'

'KK, ya – stop being so stupid. Why not just meet him?'

Why not, indeed? she thinks.

Poochie the pug suddenly dives off the sofa and races out.

His mistress, too, jumps up. 'I think Rahul's come,' Priya says. 'I'll just go down, but when I come back you have to tell me more about this guy. Come on, ya, this sounds damn exciting.' She skips out of the room.

Ketaki could make her exit now. She could feign exhaustion, and that would hardly be a lie. But if she were at her own flat, she would have to handle a more trying companion: herself.

Rahul saunters in.

'Hi,' Ketaki says.

'Oh, hi,' he replies.

'How are things?'

'Really busy.' He fixes himself a whiskey from the bar, reclines on the sofa, and switches on the television.

'Uff-o,' Priya says, as she comes in. 'Rahul, ya, have you even asked KK if she wants a drink?'

'Sorry,' he says, and kicks off his shoes.

'KK, will you have a drink?' Priya asks.

Bless you, Ketaki thinks. 'A whiskey would be fine,' she says.

'Sorry, ya, you know how men are,' Priya says, then turns to Rahul: 'Listen babes, do you know some guy called Siddharth Nanda?'

'No,' Rahul says.

'Think carefully, ya,' she pleads to Rahul. 'Siddharth Nanda. Banker type. You must know him.'

'Never heard the name.'

'Uff, then get off your lazy bum and make KK a drink.'

When she is safely returned to her flat she is drunk; not plastered to the point of passing out, as she hoped to be, but soused. She blunders her way into the bathroom, brushes her teeth, and gets into bed. Prostrate in front of the draught of the air conditioner, she waits for the miasma of intoxication around her to disperse. Before it actually does so, she sits up. She has not seen her uncle all day. Her aunt will be in bed, she thinks, cosied up to her stack of weeklies borrowed every Sunday from Live Love Learn Lending Library in Defence Colony Market. She will not bother them. Ketaki will also tell the nurse to take a break. Yes, then it will be just the two of them.

But first she will get ready for him. She will powder herself a perfect white, then proceed to her lips, which she will paint, purse, and paint again a rich and deathly red. Her hair will be bobby-pinned into place, a single kiss-curl made to rest on the left side of her face. It will be just the two of them, Deepak and her, his kabuki lover. Lover? No, Deepak and her, Ketaki: woman dressed as man dressed as woman on tiptoes.

The strings of the samisen are calling for her to begin. The hooded black figures of the kurogo have taken their hidden places. He will be lying there in concealed excitement. Maiden in the temple of repair, she must inch into the performance like a cat, and he will whistle and hoot when she enters. She must pose and posture before him, statuesque, and he will say: O! My musume! Don't tease me so! You have set me on fire, and now you douse me with the cold water of your eyes! She must lure him from the toes up, igniting cell after cell of his body with only the barest movement. Stop! he will say. Stop, my musume! And she will only stop when he cries for more.

She lies down again, her head whirls. Triple L Lending Library, she thinks, and smacks the light switch off.

4

As the car makes its way up the long gravelled driveway leading to Adil's house, 'All Out of Love' by Air Supply oozes out of the radio. Give us your tired, your tuckered, your wrinkled soft rockers, Ketaki thinks, and we Indians will make stars out of them again.

Her cellphone rings. It is her aunt.

'Where are you?' Neera says.

'In the car.'

'Oh, then never mind.'

'It's okay. I'm being driven.'

'I wanted to check if you'd be home for dinner.'

'No. I'm going out. I was going to call – '

'All right. I was just checking.'

'I was going to call you.'

'All right.'

'I'll come – '

'Good night.' Then click; Neera has hung up.

The car has stopped. Ketaki takes a moment to gather herself, to let the sudden upset in her stomach let up. She opens the car door to see Adil standing in front of her, smiling.

He holds her shoulders and kisses her on each cheek. 'A lot of traffic?' he says.

She would like him to hold her longer, then shake her, shake her hard. 'It wasn't too bad,' she says.

They walk up to the house and settle themselves in the study. She curls into a leather chair and closes her eyes.

'Could I rouse you with some wine?' he asks, standing above her.

'Sounds good.'

'I haven't tried it. It's a Chablis — something a client got for me.'

'That's fine,' she says. As long as there is enough of it, she thinks.

'Excellent. Give me a second.'

Adil returns with his bearer in tow. The wine is uncorked and decanted.

'I thought you're not meant to decant whites,' she says.

'Mostly not, but this is a young one, a French Chablis. It's better to,' he says.

'Okay, but quickly please.'

He looks up from the ritual and smiles at her. 'Maybe you're in need of something stronger,' he says.

'Maybe,' she says with a grin. 'A smack of crack or something.'

Finally, the wine is fit for consumption and poured into glasses. Adil stretches out on the sofa.

'Where's your mum?' she asks.

'She's in Hong Kong with my brother.'

'That's nice.'

'Feroz is taking her for a six-week holiday around Australia and New Zealand.'

'Six weeks?'

'That's right. High school teachers have it good.'

'They do,' she says.

'Always on vacation.'

'I guess it compensates for the low salaries.'

'His father left him enough,' Adil says, giving his wine a swirl. 'But how are you doing?'

'I'm okay,' she says. 'Well, sort of. But Deepak Uncle's not well. Not well at all.' She brings her knees up to her chest.

'I know. Your uncle, General Mehra, told me at the club the other night. I'm really sorry.'

'It's okay. He's in a coma – after a cardiac arrest.'

'I didn't bring it up because I knew you would, when you were ready.'

'I know that,' she says.

'How's your aunt?'

'My aunt? I don't know.'

'It must be diffi – '

'It's exhausting. She doesn't say a fucking word. She won't just say, Hey, I'm feeling like shit, I need help. And we never talk about what happened – or about what will happen. It's been almost a month, but not a word about it. And she goes about her life as if everything's normal. That's what's tiring. Pretending is tiring. It's difficult enough as it is, but to pretend that all's well with the world – that's fucking exhausting.'

'It must be,' Adil says.

'Or she just doesn't care.'

'Sorry?'

'I don't know. She's always been like this – she does all her wifely duties, goes through all the motions of being the good wife, but I don't think she feels very much. Anyway, we've brought him home now.'

'Home?'

She rests her head on the back of the chair. 'My aunt

54

insisted on it,' she says. 'Which is okay. He's better off at home. And we have day and night nurses.'

'If it's all right, can I ask you what actually happened?' he says.

'When?'

'To your uncle...'

'He had a cardiac arrest and went into a coma after that,' she says. She tries to think back to the moment, to build some kind of narrative, but both her memory and her storytelling faculties are struggling. 'When we were on holiday – when the three of us were in Sangla last month – he nearly drowned. He didn't die. It was a cardiac arrest. He was brought back to Delhi. Almost three weeks in hospital – or was it two? The doctors said it was hypoxia or something – severe cerebral hypoxia or something – when the brain is deprived of oxygen. There was serious damage – irreparable damage – to his brain.' She stretches out her legs. 'So he's a vegetable, he's going to be a vegetable until he dies, and if he makes it to Diwali, it's something for which we should be grateful.'

'I'm sorry,' he says.

'This wine is working miracles,' she says, lifting the glass to the light. 'Maybe the magic lies in the decanting.'

'Thank you,' he says, and takes his first sip of the evening. 'But you do know that if you need anything, or if you just need to talk, you can, you know, call me.'

'I know. Thank you.' She probably does need to talk. The fact is that she goes off on her aunt's stubborn reserve, but until this evening she herself has not spoken to a soul about this. But were she to tell him about her little tryst with her comatose uncle, how would he react? 'I'm losing my mind,' she starts, then stops.

'You're in a very difficult – '

'No, seriously. I'm losing my fucking mind.'

'It can feel like that,' Adil says. 'You're in a really difficult situation.'

'No, I think I was mucking around with my uncle,' she says. 'My dying uncle, who happens to be my dead mother's sister's husband. I sent the nurse away, I snuck about, I lay with him, I groped him, played games with him – my uncle. My comatose uncle.'

Adil picks up his wine glass.

'You're going to need that,' she says.

'Sometimes we paint ourselves into corners,' he says.

'He's in a coma.'

'I know, but sometimes we lose it. When things are beyond our coping we just lose it.'

He is choosing his words carefully, she thinks. It is as if with a philatelist's care he is picking each word up, holding it to the light, examining it from near and far. But no matter his words, no matter their comfort, the fact is that what she did with Deepak was stupid; in truth, insane. It is one thing if he were well, if he were a little more alive, but messing around with a near-dead man?

Adil takes another short sip of his wine. 'The night after my father died I took all his walking sticks and burned them. He had quite a collection – in mahogany, wenge, ebony – all very precious to him. I just grabbed them all and burned them in the driveway.'

'You were upset.'

'Six months later my wife filed for divorce.'

'That must've been awful.'

'I don't know. It was a relief too.'

'I remember you telling me that,' she says.

'I behaved appallingly,' Adil says.

'But you guys get along now. You're always meeting up with her or one of your ex-girlfriends.'

'That's true.'

'I'm sorry,' she says.

'For what?'

'All this weird shit I'm unloading on you.'

'It isn't all that weird. I don't think you should take it too seriously,' he says.

'I think we need refills,' she says.

Adil gets up, gives her a poke in the stomach, and fetches the decanter from the bar.

'You're doing a good job, you know.'

'Of what?' he asks, pouring the wine into her glass.

'Hiding your horror.'

'Horror? Please.'

'Come on.'

'Of course, it isn't something that I'd encourage,' he says, his eyes sparkling.

Together they laugh.

'Yes, I'm not sure necrophilia is constitutional,' she says.

'Probably not.' He walks over to her and sits on the arm of her chair.

'I'm tired,' she says, leaning into him.

Adil gathers her hair into a ponytail and bending down, lifts it to kiss the base of her neck. She starts. 'I'm sorry,' he says, and moves back.

'You know, this wasn't the first time,' she says.

'What wasn't the first time?'

'My uncle and I. My uncle and I messing around. It sort of happened before.'

'You never told me.'

'What would I have said?'

'True, what could you have said?' he says, getting up.

'And my aunt. I think she suspects something.'

'About what?'

'About my uncle and I.'

'In what way?'

'I don't know. She makes these little digs.' Ketaki knocks back her wine. 'How about dinner?' she says.

'Okay.'

'I need to wash my hands though.'

'Use the loo in my room.'

She hurries through his bedroom and into the bathroom, and shuts the door. Looking at her face in the mirror, she places her hand on the back of her neck where Adil tried to kiss her. She turns away from her reflection. On a slim chest of drawers near the WC is a large framed photograph of Adil's father standing next to a greyhound, which is flanked by Tony Judt's *Postwar* and two volumes on tantric sex. Weirdo, she thinks. Adil is another fucking weirdo.

After washing her hands, she comes out and sits down on the edge of his bed, then lies back. Lars thought Judt was disputatious and unreliable, she recalls. He would have baulked at the sight of *Postwar*. But how would he have reacted to the other two books? Lars liked sex. He liked sex a lot, in fact, though maybe not of the tantric kind. Her eyes close and she allows herself to travel back to scenes unvisited since she moved back: to Brooklyn, to the apartment in Carroll Gardens that Lars and she shared, to the bed on which they lay for hours day and night cracking Sudoku Xtreme puzzles and listening endlessly to Prokofiev's *The Love for Three Oranges*. How would he feel now, she wonders, knowing that Deepak is dying and can no longer intrude upon them?

Lars had known it before she did. It was he who made

her see, after much resistance and recrimination on her part, that Deepak and she shared more than what is typical of a familial bond between uncle and niece. Once she silently recognized it, once she silently accepted it, and once everything between Lars and her inevitably collapsed, she tried and failed to understand how it had come to be this way between her uncle and her. Not only was she unable to identify what exactly it was that had changed in her relationship with Deepak, she also could not pinpoint when the transformation took place. It was not as if one fine day Deepak and Ketaki looked into each other's glazed eyes and pronounced everlasting love. In reality, she has never been in love with Deepak. Neither was it that she was some young, tragic Delgadina lured by her uncle and imprisoned for rebuffing his advances. But how does the how and what and when of it matter any more? Deepak is on his way out, Lars is long gone – he has even met someone now – and she is, well, mostly okay.

Adil comes in a few minutes later. 'Are you all right?' he asks.

'I'm fine,' she says. 'Just needed a little lie-down.'

Both of them are lying on the bed now, side by side, looking up at the ceiling.

'It's getting late for dinner, isn't it?' she says.

'It's fine. Take your time.'

'I'm sorry about this. I've completely fucked up your evening.'

'It's better than being alone,' he says, 'or spending it with one of my exes.' He turns over to look at her.

'I thought you liked hanging out with them.'

'Well…' He brings his hand to her face and tucks a stray lock of her hair behind her ear. 'How's work?' he says.

'No work.'

'Did Kadambari Jayaraman email you?'

'She did, but I didn't follow up with her – I'm sorry.'

'That's okay. I just thought you might find some of her projects interesting.'

'I haven't managed to do a thing in I don't know how long,' she says, raising herself up again.

'It's all right. It'll come back.'

'The thing is when someone dies, it isn't just the person that you lose. Everything he's ever touched is lost too. It's all dead.'

Adil sits up too.

'I don't know,' she says. 'Anyway, he's not dead.'

Her phone rings. For the second time this evening it is Neera.

'Are you finished?' her aunt says.

'Finished?' Ketaki says.

'With dinner.'

'No. Is everything okay?'

'Yes, fine. Where are you?'

'At Adil's. Are you all right?'

'I'm fine. Good night.' Neera hangs up.

'All okay?' Adil asks.

'I don't know,' she says, collapsing back onto the bed. 'The woman is crazy – fucking crazy.'

'Your aunt?'

'Forget it,' she says.

Again, Adil lowers himself next to her, the full length of his body against hers.

She sits up abruptly. 'What are you doing?' she says, looking down at him. 'You want to kiss me, right? You want to fucking fuck me, don't you?'

'What?' he says, leaping up from the bed, his face terror-struck. 'I was – '

Grabbing his hand, she pulls him towards her. 'No, I'm sorry,' she says. 'Fuck, I'm so sorry. I don't know what I was thinking. Please, sit. Please.'

He plunks down beside her.

'I'm really sorry,' she says, still holding onto his hand. 'I just don't know what I'm doing.'

His head drops and his eyes fix on the bathroom door in front of them.

'Talk to me, please,' she says, after a few moments. 'Please.'

'I'm sorry,' he says.

'No. Don't be. You did nothing. I'm sorry. I'm so sorry.'

'It's okay.'

'Adil? Could you look at me?'

He turns his head in her direction.

'Look, I'm really sorry.'

'It's okay,' he says. 'I was probably out of line. I'm sorry – and you're going through a difficult time as it is.'

'No, no, I'm fine. Really, don't worry.'

A suggestion of a smile appears on his face. 'Let's have dinner,' he says.

The lights are off in the hall and the drawing room. Her aunt's bedroom, too, is in darkness.

'Masi?' she says.

There is no trace of sound or movement.

She peers into the guest bedroom, where her uncle lies like a child in the glow of the table lamp, his nurse asleep on a chair by his side. After her mother died, this was her room. As a child, she, too, lay here – if she was not lying between her aunt and uncle in the master bedroom. While her father moved from Srinagar to Hong Kong to London and finally to New York, for eight years this was her room; this place was her home with Neera and Deepak and her grandmother.

Standing in the shadows of the hall, she hears a low and constant shuffle and clink. Once she determines the direction from which the sounds come, she closes the door to her uncle's room and makes her way to the kitchen.

Just as the rest of the house has been switched off for the night, the kitchen is palpitant with activity. With her back to the door, Neera is at the counter, chopping something or other, while the microwave, the fan, the stovetop, and the oven are all in use.

'Masi,' Ketaki says.

Her aunt turns around, the expression on her face slowly shifting from blankness to surprise to, maybe, just maybe, a recognition of the ridiculousness of this midnight scene. 'What are you doing here?' Neera says.

'Why did you call me?'

Her aunt returns to the chopping board.

'Masi, look at me,' Ketaki says, her voice rising. 'Why did you call me?'

'Don't use that tone with me,' Neera says, her back still to Ketaki.

'Answer my question: Why did you call me over and over again this evening?'

Neera spins around quickly and lowers at her niece. 'So now you want reasons, now I have to justify why I call you,' she says. 'And I only called you twice.'

'Fuck this,' Ketaki says, and walks out of the kitchen.

'Don't talk to me like that,' Neera says, following her out in heavy strides. 'Where are you going?'

'Home.'

'Talk softly. Your uncle will wake up.'

'What world are you living in? My uncle – your husband, for fuck's sake – will not wake up.'

'Don't talk like that,' Neera says. 'And you've been drinking, haven't you? Drinking and smoking.'

'What's wrong with you?'

'Don't talk like that,' Neera says again. 'Let's sit in the drawing room.'

'What for?'

'Come.'

'No,' Ketaki says.

'Just for a few minutes.'

Neera puts her hand to the small of Ketaki's back and guides her through the dark towards the front of the house. She puts on the lamps in the drawing room, and they sit down hip to hip on the sofa.

'I was baking a cake for you,' Neera says, opening her right hand out to reveal a fistful of blanched almonds.

'Baking a cake at close to midnight. That makes sense.'

'I couldn't sleep.'

'Why couldn't you sleep?'

'How is Adil?'

'He's fine.'

'Good. I hear you're going to be meeting that Nanda boy.'

'I haven't thought about it.'

Neera refolds the newspaper on the coffee table.

'How is he?' Ketaki says.

'I've never met him. His father – '

'Not the Nanda guy. I'm talking about Deepak Uncle.'

'Om Prakash said that the day nurse came late.'

'She was only fifteen minutes late,' Ketaki says. 'But how is Deepak Uncle doing?'

'Fine. But this agency is totally useless. First the night nurse didn't come – she didn't even have the decency to call – and now this one comes late.'

'This was the agency the hospital recommended.'

'And she smells of coconut oil,' Neera says. 'But, you know, they're showing highlights of the cricket world cup final on TV just now. Would you like to watch them?'

'So why couldn't you sleep?' Ketaki asks again.

'Just. You know I've always had trouble sleeping. It runs in the family. The business that we have given Calmpose manufacturers – '

'Stop it.'

'You're shouting,' Neera says. 'Calm down. I know this is difficult for you.'

'For me? For me? What about you? Look at you.'

'It's difficult for everyone,' Neera says.

'Don't you feel anything? Don't you love him?'

'Love him? He's my husband,' she says.

'And?'

'And what? One has to be brave.'

'How simple.' Ketaki wants to suffocate her aunt with the brocade floor cushion or, better still, strangle her with one of the curtains' silly tassels. Sadly for both of them these delicious, irresistibly easy options die almost as soon as they are conceived.

'What else can one do?' Neera says. 'People come into your life, people go. Or pass away. One can't stop it.'

'I can't believe it. I can't believe what you're saying. You were just like this when Mummy – your sister, your only fucking sister – died. I remember you watering the flowerbeds.'

'What do you want me to do? Sit and cry? Run to the temple? Feed the poor? One has to cope with it, doesn't one? That's all one can do.'

'You call this coping?' Ketaki says. 'Your husband is lying here, here in your fucking house. But just look at yourself. How many times have you been to see him? Can you tell me?'

'Are you finished?'

'But then when have you ever cared about him?'

'Listen to me,' Neera says, standing up, 'you do whatever you want with him, but don't you dare interfere with my relationship with him.'

'What the fuck do you mean, Do whatever you want with him?' Ketaki says.

Neera swings around and walks out.

Ketaki rushes into her uncle's room. She stands at the foot of the bed; Deepak does not look at her. She pummels the metal frame of the bed; he does not stir. She charges into the bathroom, grabs the bedpan from under the sink, and hurls it at the mirror. She throws the plastic mug to the floor and herself to the wall, and slides down to a crouch on the floor. Knocking her head against her knees, rage ultimately submits to a milder form of itself and allows her to bring her breathing back to normal, get up, and wash her face.

When she comes out of the bathroom she notices Gopal Singh squatting in a dark nook near the sofa, looking out of the window. She stops short, then walks up to him with all the haughtiness she can muster. 'Where's the nurse?' she says.

'She's gone to the other room.'

'Why are you here?'

'I'm here every night.'

Ketaki sits down on the sofa. 'Why?' she says.

He turns away. Sitting in his frog pose, in the inky silence of one corner, he will not talk to her, but instead look at a moon that has now revealed itself through the latticed window, that hangs in the hush of darkness struggling to manage the swirl of time.

She leaves the room.

She cannot sleep, but it is an unremarkable condition. When did she last enjoy the kind of heady nothingness essential to rest? She gets out of bed, picks up her cigarettes and lighter, and walks out to the terrace.

The air is heavy with the threat of rain, and it is still, so still that cigarette ash she tipped on the ground the night before has remained undisturbed. On his own terrace, old Mr Chatterji is stooped over the railing under a halo of hungry mosquitoes. Her first instinct is to stub out the cigarette she has just lit – she still has strange ideas about smoking in public in India – but decides against it. Fat and shirtless, he is watching her smoke, enjoying it, perhaps. For a moment she, too, wants to be shirtless, for him, this sweet beast. The impulse, however, remains just that. She drags on her cigarette until she can feel the nicotine flush through her, until her body is in a delicious dither, then she lies down on the charpoy.

A slick of insoluble thoughts floats upon the higher thinking centres of her brain. But how can they dissolve? she thinks. They await confrontation, confrontation and resolution, and so long as she does nothing, these thoughts will stay.

She tries now, as she has tried a thousand times before, to relive the events from the moment he collapsed. In every earlier attempt at recall, she stalled at the instant when that woman with the burn scars – Malvika? Mallika? – screams. But she will try harder this time. She will take it to the end.

They are on holiday in the Sangla valley, on a birdwatching holiday. It is a perfect day in May in the mountains. Deepak is down at the river, the Baspa, to take a closer look at the White-capped Water Redstarts they had earlier spotted. The water is a fantastic blue, the colour of mouthwash. That woman, Malvika/Mallika, who is staying in the tent next to theirs, is eating a mango while perched on a boulder a few metres away from Deepak. From far and above, sitting by their Swiss tent drinking shandies, Ketaki and her aunt watch him step on stones, dip his toes into the water, plunge in, float a bit, disappear, come up, disappear again. They see the woman stand up, and then, from out of nowhere, a man appears. They see the man run to Deepak, or rather, slip, slide, fall, and get up again, over and over, until he manages to grab Deepak. They watch closely, but like the boulders, the deodar, the mountains around them, they do not move.

And then she screams. The woman whose face from the nose down is a tableau of burn and reconstruction screams, and Neera grips Ketaki's arm, and the woman comes scrambling up the riverbank, and tells them that she will fetch the resort owner, and not to worry, she has contacts in the army, and she will arrange for a medical unit, and it will be fine, they will be here in no time at all, and everything will be fine. Then what? Medical help probably arrives, but Ketaki cannot see it. She does recall some grim chatter about cardiac arrest and defibrillation and cardiopulmonary resuscitation – resuscitation, what a joke – and medivac procedures. And then he is in Delhi, at Apollo Hospital, for days and days at Apollo Hospital, and now he is back home, and now this, her, without sleep, lying on her terrace in the purr of the night, going through the motions of remembering in the hope that she will feel better.

Winter

5

There are some things about your family that you know in your bones; you come to life with the information, and from first breath your understanding of the world is shaped by it. You are shaped by it. Then there are secrets, family secrets, which have been held tight among a knowing few for years. Often they remain so, as hidden truths and hidden lies withheld for generation upon generation. Occasionally they are shared. As Ketaki fast approaches her twenty-ninth birthday such an occasion has arisen. It is January, and her father is visiting from New York. He came over to her flat this afternoon to talk.

I know this is a very difficult time, Vikram began, as they sat in the winter sun on her terrace. Both for you and Neera. But you must understand that with Deepak in this condition you and Neera only have each other here. You cannot let anything come between the two of you. I know she can be tough, but she hasn't had an easy life.

And then Vikram told her a story.

As you know, in the winter of '86 the bank posted me to Srinagar, her father said. Your mummy wasn't happy to leave Delhi, but it was a prestigious posting and important for my career. After a lot of persuasion she agreed to move the following summer. She didn't want to come immediately.

She said the Kashmir winter would be too cold for you. You were not even eight then. I set up the house, I arranged for your school admission, but six months later I got a call from her saying your nanima was very ill. She said she couldn't leave her. But she brought you to Srinagar for Diwali and we had a gala time together. Do you remember cracking walnuts in the door hinges? And you loved the mountains even then, you know. You were so intrigued by them. Do they grow like trees? you would ask. Are they the biggest things in the whole wide world? Do you remember how you would sit out in the garden all afternoon trying to paint them? How you would always be so upset that the paper was not large enough for the mountains you wanted to paint? They don't fit, Papa, you would say. I need the biggest paper in the whole wide world. Do you remember?

After that another few months passed, but your mummy still didn't come. I was quite lonely, I missed you both dearly. But I didn't think much of it. I thought sooner or later she would move to Srinagar with you. And I tried to keep myself busy with work and tennis and golf. Do you remember the golf course in Gulmarg? Then in January the following year, when I came down to Delhi for your ninth birthday, Neera said she needed to talk to me. She was in very bad shape, the poor lady. We went for a drive. And then she told me.

She said people were talking. She said she had known all along, but now people were talking. People had seen them around. At a coffee shop, at the Rose Garden. I kept quiet. I let her say what she wanted to say. I kept driving. It was about your mummy and Deepak.

She said she had first noticed it in '81 – seven years earlier – but she thought it was a passing phase. It wasn't. Your mummy and Deepak continued to carry on. Neera said she never wanted to tell me, but since people were talking she thought it was her duty to tell me.

Of course it came as a great shock to me. We had been married eighteen years. I knew your mummy was a vivacious lady, very pretty and very vivacious, and she got a lot of attention from everyone. I knew she and Deepak were always very friendly, but I thought that it was because they were childhood friends that they acted like that – their families were neighbours in Babar Lane after Partition. I did not believe there was a deeper attraction. Then I talked to your mummy. I asked her if what Neera said was true. She said it was.

I couldn't understand it, Ketu. I thought we had a wonderful marriage – eighteen years of it. She seemed happy. I didn't know I was lacking in something, or making her unhappy. She never said anything to that effect. She seemed happy as my wife. Really, when I was in Srinagar, she would call me all the time. I thought she missed me as I missed her.

I tried a lot to ask her about it but she would not reveal very much. She said the reason was not me. She even said she still had feelings for me. Then why? I asked, and she was quiet. Each time I tried to ask her she would become quiet. She said she had no answers. I was completely at a loss. And then I just could not believe Deepak could have done this. Do you remember the way Deepak was with you? Do you remember? He adored you, you adored him. Really, I would have to check myself because I often found myself feeling jealous of the bond you both shared. I could not believe he would do something that could hurt you. I tried to ask Neera but she just would not talk about it, and I didn't want to probe as she was also in a terrible way. But really, I could not understand why all this had happened.

Your mummy and I didn't talk about divorce or such matters. In those days it was different. I returned to Srinagar then, both of you remained in Delhi, and we would meet every few months because I wanted to see you. I tried to spend as much time as I could with you, I think you wanted to spend time with me too. And I still wanted to be with her. I tried to woo her back. But it was no use. Barely a year after the talk with Neera, she was dead.

I was very upset then. I was upset with your mummy, I was upset with Deepak. When I saw him weeping over her when she died, I felt very angry. I didn't talk to him, I didn't talk to him for two years, I think. But in the end I think I forgave them both. Everyone makes mistakes. And sometimes there are no reasons, no explanations.

I don't know what happened between Neera and Deepak. She and I have never spoken about it after that day in the car. I don't know if she confronted him, I don't know what he might have said. All I know is they continued to live together as man and wife.

Betrayal is a complicated thing, Ketu. People respond differently. I was very upset and angry for a while, but in the end you have to be positive. You know, today I feel blessed. I have a loving partner Megan, I have a good job, and, most importantly, I have a wonderful daughter. What more can a man ask for? But for Neera it has been difficult. I don't think she has made her peace with it, poor lady. I tried to talk to her on quite a few occasions, but she never let me broach the subject. But then we all handle situations differently.

All I want to say is we should not judge people too quickly. We don't know what they have been through, what has made them the way they are. Neera has had a difficult life, and we shouldn't be too hard on her. I know she can act a little oddly with you at times, but you have to understand her circumstances, and all said and done, she loves you like her own child. If it wasn't for her, I don't know what would have happened. I could not be in Delhi. I tried, but it was very difficult, and it was decided you should stay with Neera and Deepak, and you seemed fine with that. Really, after your mummy died, she was the one who looked after you. She loves you. And the same goes for your mummy and Deepak. Whatever they may have done, they're otherwise fine people, fine people who've loved you very much.

One moment a heart liquid with longing over Deepak freezes. The next moment it thaws again for her father and her aunt. As for her dead mother, she feels nothing at all. But then, has she ever?

Vikram has left the flat. He was quiet after he finished, possibly awaiting some reaction from his daughter, but the only non-violent response she could think of, once she was able to think, was to tell him that she needed to be alone. Thankfully, he went away quietly.

Now, as clouds collect thick and gold above her, she remains on the terrace, lying upon the charpoy. When she notices that the rain has begun to fall, she goes back inside. She thinks of calling Adil, then decides against it. She considers going across to her aunt's, but that, too, she cannot do. After a hot bath she gets into bed.

Twenty-nine years need to be imagined again; it is as if an entire history demands to be rewritten. There are some things about family that should remain secret.

•

Underneath a breadth of stars, men and women take their morning walks, truckers bolt their roadside breakfasts by weary fires, little children in oversized blazers wait for their school buses. She drives slowly towards Gurgaon in the imperfect black of this winter morning.

It was another night of half-sleep; an extended hypnagogic state in which her mother and father, Deepak, Neera, Lars, and Adil marched in and out of her head in an endless procession. By three thirty she had had enough and got out of bed. She spent an hour pottering around the house, checking email, playing a dismal round of online Scrabble and countless games of Capsule on her cellphone. Then she called Krishan.

Krishan is the only person she knows who is up at five. He is also the only person with whom she shares a relationship that cannot be touched by what was revealed to her yesterday. Every other relationship, every other attachment that she has must now be reconfigured based on her father's disclosure. But with Krishan, her past – her new past – has no bearing because there is no future with him.

And then there are no questions. With Krishan there are never any questions. She could at this very instant turn the car around and go home, and he probably would not phone to find out why she did not show up as she had said she would. Even when she called him at four in the morning asking to see him, he did not try to wrest an explanation from her. Sure, yaar, he said. But come quickly, I have to go to the gym at six thirty. As simple as that.

She pulls over once she passes the Haryana border post and dials him.

'Are you downstairs?' Krishan says.

'No. At the border.'

'Huh?'

'Let's meet here.'

'Why, yaar? You were going to come to the office.'

'I don't feel like driving any further.'

'Oh-ho, I will pick you up from there.'

'No. I have to get back soon.'

'Why?'

'It's okay then. We can meet some other time.'

'Okay, okay, wait. I am just coming.'

Krishan parks his car a hundred or so metres from hers. She watches him manoeuvre his lovely lithe body dressed in black top-to-toe out of his small red Santro, turn slowly a la Salman Khan, and stride towards her, hand in pocket, smiling. He opens the door to the passenger seat of her car, shakes her hand, and sits down.

'Happy? Anything you command, I do,' he says, offering her a full display of his teeth.

'Yes, thank you.'

'So...' he says, reclining back on the car seat with his legs set wide apart, 'how are you?'

'Fine.'

'It looks like you have been partying a lot,' he says, grinning. 'Look at your eyes, yaar. All-night discoing, huh?'

'How's business?' she says, fixing her slouch.

'Not bad. A lot of contracts, man – outstation contracts. My daddy will handle those ones, and I will handle the Delhi ones. He still thinks I am too young to manage all. But it is good.'

'Good.'

'And what about you?'

'It's going well, thanks,' she says.

'I like your life, man,' Krishan says. 'See, you don't have to worry about anything. And see, anything you do, your father is cool.' He raps the dashboard with his fingers. 'If I don't do what my daddy says, he will throw me out of the business – he will even throw me out of the house.'

'But you're happy...'

'Ya, that is true. So far so good.'

'Thank you for coming.'

'No problem. So, you want to come to the office now?' He swings one leg over the other.

'No, not now.'

'Just you and me...' he says, looking down at his pectorals. His nipples pierce through the T-shirt stretched tightly across his chest.

'No. I'm sorry.'

'So... you want... you want to talk?'

She smiles.

Krishan's foot shakes in short rapid movements. 'So, my sister is getting married,' he says.

'Congratulations. When?'

'Ya, but my turn next.' He rotates his neck, clockwise first, then anti-clockwise. 'Daddyji says a boy must get married by twenty-six.'

'When's the wedding?'

'November.'

'That's not far. The shopping and preparations must have started.'

'We have booked the hall. Her trousseau is also done.'

'Your parents must be happy.'

'Ya, it is good,' he says, examining his right biceps, biceps worked to perfection. 'She is at a marriageable age.'

'You only have two years to go. You better start looking.'

He grins. 'You are also at a marriageable age,' he says.

'You probably think I'm past it.'

'But your family is modern. Your father has a foreign girlfriend, and your masi and uncle are so cool… Yaar, no one pressurizes you.'

'You don't want to get married?'

'No, no, of course I do. But first I have to settle down in the business.'

'I'm sure you'd get any girl you wanted.'

'Stop it, yaar,' he says, his eyes now small, shining. 'You are making me conscious.'

She smiles again.

'We will see. So how is your daddy?'

'He's here at the moment.'

'In India?'

'Yes.'

'Holiday?'

'Sort of. He's here to see my masi.'

'What happened to her?'

'My uncle is in a coma.'

'What happened to him?'

'He had an accident.'

'When? You never told me.'

'In June.'

'Seven months of coma?'

'Yes.'

'A lot of bad things are happening,' says Krishan, staring at his feet as if he has discovered them for the first time.

'I guess so.' She turns away to look out at the field of low-rise buildings that are coming into view through the morning smog. 'It's my birthday today,' she says.

'Really?' Krishan says. 'Wow, man, happy birthday.' He leans across, hugs her, and lets her go.

'Thank you.'

'How are you celebrating?'

'Probably go out for dinner or something.'

'Five star?'

'I don't know.'

He looks out of the window. 'So you don't want to come over?' he says.

'No. And I have to leave soon.'

'Okay.'

'But should we go for a quick drive first?' she asks.

'Drive?'

'Let's go to that hilly spot on the Faridabad road.'

'You want to go there?'

'We might catch the sun rising. It'll be lovely.'

'Okay, man. Let us go.'

'Thank you.'

He reaches across and squeezes her thigh. 'You are a mad chick, madam,' he says.

From Gurgaon she drives straight to Neera and Deepak's to have breakfast. Om Prakash greets her in the driveway. 'Happy birthday, Baby,' he says, as he hoses down the car.

'Thank you,' she says.

'How many years has it been? Twenty-eight, no?'

'Twenty-nine.'

'Twenty-nine years. You know, after your parents, I was the first one who held you. I was the one who drove you back home.'

She knows. On the twenty-fourth of January of every year that she has been in Delhi, he has never failed to claim this fact.

'Beautiful child. You were a beautiful child. And when you cried you always asked for me. You always wanted to be taken for a drive in Deepak Sahib's car. The white Ambassador – do you remember?'

'I remember it. I gave you a lot of trouble, didn't I?'

'No, no, not at all,' Om Prakash says. 'But now you go in and seek Sahib's blessings.'

Gopal Singh opens the front door and presents her with his annual smile. It is always a special present, she thinks. So much better than the recycled gift that is whored around, or the unimaginative n plus one rupees that is gifted in a hideously designed envelope. She comes into the house and pauses outside the guest bedroom, where Neera sits wrapped in her shawl with her morning tea and newspaper, while Deepak is being prettied up for the day by his nurse. Walking quietly past them to the spare bedroom, she knocks and enters to find her father cross-legged on the carpet in meditation.

'Hello there, my birthday girl,' Vikram says, opening his eyes and slowly getting up from the floor. He pulls out an envelope from his kurta pocket and hugs her. 'This is for you.'

'Thank you,' she says.

'You're awake very early,' he says. 'I thought I would wait till ten to come over.'

'I decided to join you for breakfast.'

'Thank you, my darling. Some tea?'

'Not right now, thanks.'

'Have you met Neera?'

'No, not yet.' She goes into the bathroom.

'Deepak had a bad night,' Vikram says as she comes out. 'He was very restless.'

'Have you said anything to her?' she says.

'Pardon?'

'Does Masi know I know?'

'No, Ketu, she doesn't,' he says. 'I haven't said anything to her about our conversation.'

'Okay.' She takes off her shoes and slips into bed.

'I am so sorry that I put you through this, but – '

'No, it's good. It's good you told me.'

'I just wanted you to understand Neera. I wanted you to understand why she sometimes reacts the way she does.'

'I know. It's okay. It's just that I'm... I don't know.'

'What is it, Ketu?'

'I don't know.'

'My darling, obviously this has disturbed you – and that's natural. But it's all in the past. It's over.'

'I'm a little scared. I'm scared of how... I don't know.'

'Ketu, please... What do you have to be scared of? This has got nothing to do with you. She has always loved you, always taken care of you. You're like her own child.'

She takes her cellphone out of her bag and starts playing a game of Capsule.

'Neera might have had problems with your mummy, but never with you,' Vikram says. 'Ketu? Are you listening?'

'Could we have breakfast please?' she says.

Neera greets her in the dining room with a token hug and another envelope. 'From Deepak Uncle and me,' she says, and sits down at the table.

'Thank you,' Ketaki says.

'So what are we doing today?' Vikram says, looking first at Ketaki, then at her aunt. 'I was thinking of Wasabi at the Taj Man Singh – the chef is supposed to be the Iron Chef fellow who also worked at Nobu in New York. But if the ladies have any other place in mind, I would be happy to oblige.'

Neera has no verbal or nonverbal response to offer.

'Wasabi's supposed to be ridiculously expensive,' Ketaki says.

'It's your birthday,' her father says. 'It's all right to splurge on a special occasion. What do you think, Neera?'

'That's fine.'

Ketaki looks up at her aunt, at the vertical lines between her eyebrows on an otherwise wrinkle-free face. She will be sixty this year, but she has no laugh lines or crow's feet to speak of; only two deep furrows borne of despair that divide her forehead in half. It is the life you live that makes your face, Ketaki thinks, much more than your age.

'Would you like to call anyone else?' Vikram says. 'Maybe Adil? I haven't seen him in a long time. How is he doing?'

'He's well. Busy.'

'Wouldn't you like to call him? Or what about Priya and her husband?'

'No, that's okay.'

'All right, then. I will call and make a reservation.'

Dinner was more pleasant than she had expected, and this she largely owed to her father, who kept the conversation buoyed with banter about volatile weather patterns, Bobby Jindal's victory in Louisiana, Iraq, and so forth. Neera, to be fair, tried to be as engaged – and as engaging – as she possibly could, although at one stage she stiffened when Megan called to wish Ketaki. This, however, was not a reaction that surprised anyone. For reasons that have always remained a mystery, Megan has been a taboo subject in the Sood household ever since Vikram first brought her to India eight years ago.

Adil called too. There were several calls from him during the day that she did not take; she could not bring herself to talk to him. She feared that she would let things slip, and the brittle calm of the day would be shattered. But she took his call at the restaurant. The company of her father

83

and aunt was excuse enough to keep the conversation with him short.

This is her first birthday in Delhi without Deepak. Last year it was the four of them: Ketaki and Deepak, Vikram and Neera. They drove out of Delhi, crossed Gurgaon, and found themselves a picnic spot amidst a field of mustard flowers. It was her uncle's idea. He always had ideas.

She tries to recall her ninth birthday, the occasion on which Neera spoke to her father about their spouses. What comes to mind is a shopping expedition for her birthday party to buy return presents for her friends. Deepak was driving the white Ambassador with her mother by his side, Ketaki was lying down on the backseat as she always loved to do, and they were all playing Twenty Questions. She can see it clearly, her lovely mother with her lovely hair braided into a thick, long plait laughing as Deepak and Ketaki asked funny questions in exaggerated French and Japanese and Tamil accents. But where was her father? If he had especially come down for her birthday, why was he not in that driver's seat? Was he, at that very time, in another car being told that his wife was fucking his brother-in-law? And why was Deepak there? Did he actually want to be a part of her birthday excitement or did he simply use the occasion as an excuse to be with her mother? What were the two of them doing in the front? Were they holding hands? Was he stroking her thigh? Was she giving him a handjob? Back then cars only had bench seats in the front – she could not see a thing.

Or perhaps she sees too much. Perhaps her father was driving Ketaki and her mother to buy the party favours and they sang 'There was an old lady who swallowed a fly' all the way to Khan Market. Who knows? Memory is servile, taking on the powers of the imagination to perform only as commanded.

6

It is an unusual winter afternoon in Delhi. The month-long smog lingering over the city has lifted, magically, and the lawn dazzles in the sun, as if each blade of grass has been painstakingly buffed to a mirror finish. Stupefied after three Bloody Marys and a meal suited only to a robust Punjabi constitution, she is draped over a wrought-iron garden chair, watching the brilliant metallic plumage of a Purple Sunbird in the tree to her left. She and her father are at Prakash and Usha's for lunch. Neera was invited as well, but she declined at the last minute.

'So, Keta, how is the graphic design business?' Prakash says.

'It's going okay,' Ketaki says.

'Ketaki is working on a special series of book covers for a leading independent publisher in Australia,' Vikram says. 'It's a very prestigious project – designers around the world competed for it.'

'Oh, very good, very good,' her uncle says.

Dread begins to build like bile in her stomach. She has only managed to complete one of the nine covers and her deadline is barely a fortnight away.

'Very nice,' Usha says, 'but Keta dear, do you remember our chat about Siddharth? Vijay Nanda's son?'

Ketaki tries to sit up. 'Yes, vaguely,' she says.

'Well, have you thought about it?'

Ketaki glances over at her father.

'Ketu, please don't look at me – I have nothing to do with this,' Vikram says.

'Keta dear,' Usha says, 'you must have an open mind. I know it did not work out with Madhu Rai's son, but I tell you, this Nanda boy is well and truly a lovely boy. I mean if I had an unmarried daughter, I would just grab him.'

Ketaki smiles; she is not quite sure how to respond to her aunt and uncle. She certainly does not want to encourage this, but she knows that a flat-out no will only escalate the onslaught.

'See, dear,' Usha continues, 'don't look at it as some arranged marriage sort of thing. This is not at all like that. And as we promised, there will be no parents involved. Vijay and Shireen Nanda are very broadminded people. Just like us.'

'And Siddharth has an MBA from Stanford University. Mummy?' Prakash says, turning to Usha.

'He's very well-educated and, I tell you, so well-mannered,' Usha says. 'And he has a very good job here. Six-figure dollar salary, dear.'

Ketaki looks to her father, who can only react with a smile.

'And we have told your father about Mrs Nanda,' Usha says, 'We told him she is Muslim but not to worry, she doesn't wear any hijaab-shijaab, and he says that is just fine. Tell her, Vikram.'

'That's true. I have no problem with Mrs Nanda being Muslim.'

'Then tell her, no, Vikram. Convince her to meet him.'

'It's entirely up to Ketu,' he says. 'And in any case, I don't think her problem is with Mrs Nanda's religion.'

'Then what is the problem, Keta?' Usha says. 'Arranged marriage? But, dear, we have all been through it and see

86

how wonderful it is. And we're not asking you to make a decision in twenty-four hours like we had to do. In our time, I tell you, we had to, but times are changing – '

'Oh, I still remember when your papa came to meet Uma at home,' Prakash says. 'We were all there – Papaji and Ma, of course, and Neera and Deepak and myself. Vikram, do you remember that time? You wore a three-piece suit in July! But obviously it worked. You know, Keta, he was such a hit. He was such a hit with all of us, not just your mummy. Deepak and I hit it off so well with your papa that after the tea party we went to the club for drinks. The three of us were inseparable – beer, golf, cricket, movies, holidays together. What a time...'

'Yes, but as I was saying,' Usha says, 'we are only suggesting you both meet. After that it is the boy and girl's decision. No pressure from parents. All we will do is give him your number. Then he will call you, and you both can meet independently. The oldies will not interfere. But, of course, we will not give him your number until you give us permission to. Not at all. No, Daddy?'

Prakash shakes his head in intense agreement.

'We respect how you feel,' Usha says.

Ketaki plays with her silver pendant, a birthday gift from Lars. She remembers now the red lacquered box in which it came, how Lars had left it in the bathtub for her to discover.

'So, dear, can we?'

'Let me think about it.'

'Of course, of course, please think. Don't feel any pressure,' Usha says. 'But, I tell you, thinking too much is also not good.'

•

'I'm sorry about that,' Vikram says, as they drive home from lunch.

'It's okay,' Ketaki says. 'So what do you think?'

'That's hardly the question we should be asking. You tell me, how do you feel about it?'

'I don't know. Look, be a little paternal, please – act like a father. Help me, advise me, guide me. You never say anything.' Her hold on the steering wheel tightens.

'I'm sorry, Ketu, sometimes I'm afraid of being a meddling father,' he says, resting his hand on her shoulder. 'But I don't think there is any harm in meeting him. Meeting him doesn't bind you to anything.'

She is surprised at herself, surprised that she is so much as even entertaining the idea of a set-up – an arranged marriage – let alone having a conversation about it with her father. This is not the first time such a proposal has been made to her; many similar tenders have come her way in the past – never from Vikram or Neera and Deepak, thankfully – and although most of them she shot down at first mention, she succumbed on two occasions, which, predictably, ended in disaster.

'So if you're asking for my opinion, I think you should consider it,' Vikram says. 'If you like each other, it would be wonderful, and if not, put it down to experience – or a nice free meal.' He ruffles her hair.

'True,' Ketaki says, with a short shrug of the shoulders.

'You know, when it came to your mummy, I knew I wanted to marry her the first time we met,' Vikram says. 'And she, she used to say she instantly knew I would be her husband. She said she knew it the minute she saw me walk into the drawing room of Papaji's house. Of course, at Grindlays Bank we had to seek permission to marry from Head Office in London. You will probably be shocked to hear that in the old Grindlays, every young officer – it was an all-male officer cadre in those days – but every young officer was required to submit an application with a detailed bio-data of his intended bride and family for approval from London. Your mummy and her family, of course, were considered very respectable, and the application was readily accepted. And really, your mummy was so popular with the senior Grindlays wives.'

'Do you realize that you've almost never talked about Mummy?' Ketaki says, as she makes a left on Outer Ring Road. 'Other than a couple of days ago when you dropped the bomb and now, you and I have barely had any conversation about her. And Masi too. It was only Deepak Uncle who'd talk to me about her.'

'Ketu...'

'Of course, now I know why.'

'I'm sorry.'

'It's okay. I've never really asked about her much either.'

'I'm sorry.'

'Why do you think that is?' she says. 'Why have I never really cared about her?'

'Ketu, of course you care about her.'

'I don't know.'

'You know, I really had to think a lot about whether to tell you about your mummy or not. Sometimes I thought I should let bygones be bygones. At other times I thought it was important for you to know. But – '

'But you had to wait for Deepak Uncle to be gone to do that.'

With the exceptions of Adil, whom she met through Priya, and Krishan, who came to do a waterproofing job for her flat, she has met no one new in the two years she has been in Delhi. She once briefly conversed with a postal clerk about a registered letter and she talked to the traffic policeman who fined her for an expired car pollution certificate, but other than that she has not had any noteworthy human interchange outside her dismally small circle of family and friends. It is not as if she suffers from any form of avoidant personality disorder; the problem, she is convinced, lies in the strict rules of interaction that govern public spaces in India. If she were strolling about Connaught Place or taking a walk in Lodhi Gardens, she could engage in social exchanges related to sex, for instance, or foreign currency, or illegal substances, or train tickets to avoid day-long waits at the reservation counters. But if, say, while loitering about Lodhi Gardens, she were struck by how a man looked intently at the eight piers of the Athpula Bridge, she could not simply go up to him and begin a conversation on its provenance in the hope of getting to know him. The Indian public space does not provide an interface for the kind of social activity that she is seeking.

This, then, leaves her with three choices: she could meet someone through a friend at a bar or a party – good girls never go on their own, and she is, mostly, a good girl – through work, or through groups held together by a common interest or cause – film or book discussion groups, birdwatching groups, consumer rights groups, etc. But given that she has only about two and a half friends, and she is a freelance designer who likes to keep her private and professional lives separate, and she shirks community activities in general, she has not a chance in hell of meeting anyone. So why not graciously accept the matchmaking services so generously offered by her uncle and aunt?

Yes, why not? she asks herself.

One reason could be that she has already availed of these pro bono services on two occasions and both were washouts. Has she forgotten Neel? And what about Madhav? Although the experience with Madhav was vastly different from the one with Neel, both began as set-ups and ended in collapse.

Madhav Sikand was suggested to her by Neera's Scrabble partner Prem Malhotra. Her aunt stayed out of it, but for weeks and weeks Mrs Malhotra worked on Ketaki until she agreed to meet him. He was a pleasant enough fellow, slightly built with a nascent paunch and a closely trimmed French beard. A fairly successful chartered accountant, he bought her roses, he bought her pastries, he even bought her a special number (7777) for the licence plate of her new car and had it designed in a fancy serif font. There was little that was offensive about him.

But there was also very little that was remarkable. He was just one of an undistinguished species of good Punjabi boys from good Punjabi families – a well-brought-up, unthinking, unquestioning fellow, who was not necessarily looking for love and companionship for himself as much as he was looking for love and companionship for his mummy and daddy and aunties and uncles – and Ketaki called it quits after about a month and a half. Madhav was on the whole all right with the break-up; his mother was not. Ketaki was then subjected to a series of phone calls from Mrs Sikand that started on a coaxing note and concluded with skimpily veiled threats. The calls ended only when the lady managed to find another match – a more charming, more suitable, far more respectable match – for her son three weeks later.

A couple of months after the Madhav incident, Prakash and Usha told her about their neighbour Madhu Rai's son Neel, who had recently been posted to Delhi from Singapore as South Asia bureau chief of a leading international news magazine. Again, after some cajoling, Ketaki relented. Now Neel, though also of Punjabi stock, showed no real signs of the handicaps specific to the modern Indian male. He did not care so much about what his mother thought – the woman had to be exciting to him – and he did not bother about what she did or wore or said – so long as it fell in line with his definition of cool: reading Borges and Bolaño, eating slow food, wearing Diesel denim, talking geopolitics.

For the first week or two, Ketaki and Neel met every day, made witty and worthwhile conversation, had good sex, and ate great food. He made big and small promises: I will be with you and only lovely you; I'll take you to my favourite bookshop in Darya Ganj on Saturday; Blow Delhi! We'll fly to Udaipur for New Year's Eve; and suchlike. She fell for it willy-nilly – she was susceptible. But at the last minute his colleague flew in from Hanoi and so his weekend was completely full. Then something suddenly came up and he had to fly off to Bangkok for New Year's Eve. And so on. Soon enough, they found themselves having several discussions about the verity and merit of the say-what-you-mean, mean-what-you-say truism. She also told him she could manage her expectations well, as long as he did not go about hoisting them to levels that he simply could not meet – another threadbare concept but at times there is so little else to offer. During each of these chats he assured her that he saw her point and would try to change some of his ways. He said that his problem was inconsistency, but that it was in no way symptomatic of how he felt about her, and he asked if they could start over. They started over a dozen times until, finally, it came to her with elegant though slightly painful clarity that it was time to put an end to it. His assurances seemed shallow, and even if they were not, he did not have the means to stand by them.

Her decision did not break Neel's heart, although it was a kick in the teeth. Wow, he said. Why? I guess I fucked up. And here I thought things were going really great. You're probably the only Indian woman I know who understands me. Are you sure about this? She nodded, smiled, and, wow, stood her ground.

So why this sudden shift now? she thinks.

She is bathed and dressed for bed, but the miracle of sleep sidesteps her. Wrapped in a Kullu shawl, she walks through the terrace and into the studio. She turns on the lights and the electric rod heater and the computer. Only ten days remain, and she still has eight book covers to design.

The brief she received from the Sydney publishers has nine short descriptions of nine works of literary fiction by nine – all nine – gorgeous men and women of East European extraction. The implication is clear: they want covers that reflect the serious, edgy, subversive, experimental qualities of the oh-so highbrow literature that they publish.

She has the treatment figured out already: collage. Everyone is a sucker for collage. For the first cover she used an illustration of a crow that she had done last year, which, along with a photograph of an eggbeater and scanned petals of marigold, she set against a blood red background. She sent it across to them and they loved it. But now what? To come up with a cover design based on a hundred-odd words and a pretty face is not that easy.

As she stands in front of the shelving unit in search of an idea – even a pinch of inspiration – for the next book cover, her eyes settle on the two bottom-most shelves, which hold box upon box of her mother's work. She pulls out one of them and places it on the carpet. The carton she has chosen contains a series of paintings in watercolour and gouache on A 2-sized sheets of paper. The central figure in each work is a woman, and from her emanate children and flowers and fish and mythical creatures, much like a Tree of Life image. The two-dimensional forms and a palette reminiscent of Matisse render the paintings both surrealist and childlike. Ketaki's style is very different to that of her mother's, but she can well see the talent in the work. In truth, she is nothing if not amazed by the complexity, the bold transgressions of space, and, finally, the beauty of Uma's paintings.

Gopal Singh showed up at Ketaki's doorstep with these boxes a month ago. This is for you, he had said. Madam has sent them. Since he did not disclose any further details, Ketaki was compelled to ask her aunt about them. I was organizing the garage, Neera said. A lot of your uncle's things were there that needed to be discarded and I found your mother's art pieces. That was it, that was all she divulged, and Ketaki, at the time, was in a such a rage over how her aunt acted like Deepak was already dead that she refused to open the boxes; she refused to pronounce her uncle dead.

She may have been too upset to open the boxes then, but what about now, now that the secret about her uncle and her mother is out, now that she can see why her aunt may have wanted her uncle dead, now that she might want her uncle dead too?

No, she will still not open any more boxes. She has no use for her mother's work. She only has questions.

What else did you find? Ketaki might wish to ask her aunt. Love letters? A lock of your sister's hair? And how do you feel? But as if Neera would tell her. As if Neera would seat her niece down by her side, take her hand in hers, and pour her heart out to her. Why would she want to talk about her sister banging her husband to someone whom she thinks might be guilty of the same thing? And what purpose would it serve either of them to talk? Sympathy? The gift of sympathy assumes a fundamental unity between the giver and receiver, which Ketaki and her aunt do not share, and anyway, Ketaki cannot see how a demonstration of pity could make either party feel any better.

There are questions for her father too. He needs to explain why no mention has ever been made to her about this. Ketaki can remember some of the book covers her mother did, and an odd painting or two. But boxes and boxes of them? Why has her father never told her about this? Or does he not know? Could it be that this was Deepak and Uma's special little secret? Or perhaps her father does know and is waiting for her thirtieth birthday to present her with another story?

She steps out onto the terrace. Leaning over the railing, she lights a cigarette. For someone who suffers from low peripheral circulation and who shuts down in the cold, she barely notices the chill of this winter night. But huddled in a shawl and a monkey-cap on his cane chair, old Mr Chatterji is observable, as are the moonlit clouds shirred in the old sky.

7

'So I'm meeting that guy Siddharth Nanda today,' she says to her aunt as they finish lunch. 'I decided to go ahead with it.'

'Yes,' Neera says, as she puts down her fork and picks up the napkin ring. 'Prakash Bhapa told me.'

'When did he tell you?'

'When he came over to say goodbye to your father.'

'And you didn't think you should talk to me about it?' Ketaki says.

'You never brought it up,' Neera says. 'Another chapati?'

'So what do you think?'

'Can Thomas clear the table?'

'So do you think it's a good idea?'

'What is?' Neera rolls the napkin ring around her plate.

'The set-up,' Ketaki says, trying to fight a sudden urge to hurl the jug of water in front of her at her aunt.

'You tell me,' Neera says, and rings the little silver bell for Thomas.

'I don't know. It might be nice to be with someone.'

'Well, you need to decide whether there's room for another someone in your life.'

Ketaki slams her fist down on the table.

'Why are you getting upset?' Neera says, taking the napkin off Ketaki's lap and folding it. 'But anyway, if that's what you want, if you are actually keen to get married, you might as well do it quickly. One shouldn't be so certain of one's future. One shouldn't delay things indefinitely.'

Ketaki pushes her chair back and stands up.

'Will you be home for dinner?' her aunt says.

Siddharth called three days ago, within four hours of her telling Prakash that she would meet him. She was a little suspicious about his promptness, but quickly checked her infantile reaction. They agreed upon meeting over afternoon coffee – lunch or dinner could be too long an engagement.

She knows that she is nervous. Since lunch, she has taken out piles of clothes from the cupboard, and folded and refolded them. Now she plays game after game of Capsule on her cellphone – a dead giveaway. Meeting a strange man is really not the issue. Meeting a strange man and drawing his interest is also not too much of a problem – she is a woman, she has a large albeit quite attractive Punjabi arse and tits that are not too small, and she can make all kinds of conversation. The trouble comes after the first meeting, when she tries to successfully play out what that first meeting promised. Or is there some other problem? A problem called Deepak?

She is being a little hard, though. Whatever her aunt might insinuate, whatever doubts she herself might have, she has had some fulfilling relationships. Case in point: Lars. But then Lars was exceptional. She loved other men despite themselves – despite their oddities, their shortcomings; she loved Lars because of them. Granted that he was hot and smart and kind, and listened as if she were Callas and ate her like mangosteen, but she loved him because of his protracted slowness, because of the hollows in the base of his back, because he did not shake or wipe when he pissed, and let a single drop of urine glisten and dally at the tip of his cock before it made its death landing on the floor.

Then Deepak came to visit.

But can Deepak be blamed for all her debacles? He was certainly not responsible for the misadventures with Madhav or Neel. In point of fact, whether she was fulminating over Neel not showing up for dinner or fretting about how dull Madhav was, her uncle tried hard to calm her down and offer balanced advice. She and Deepak would go for long walks on the fitness trail behind Panchsheel when she was feeling particularly lousy. Have a fag, he would start by saying – fag – that always made her smile – and she would light up. Once she pulled on her cigarette a few times, he would put his arm around her and say, Okay, now tell me. She would then embark upon a long rant that usually started with a specific complaint about the man in question and ended in a tirade against men in general.

Deepak would listen to it all with nanny-like patience. When she finished, they would sit down on a bench by the parallel bars, silently looking ahead at the dusty trees, until he pivoted on his bottom and directly addressed her profile. Sweetu, he would begin in a conciliatory voice, as if he were apologizing for all his kind, and then launch into a monologue that essentially argued that there really is no such thing as an ideal companion, and successful relationships are based on compromise but that you must carefully choose what it is that you are willing to compromise. She always came away soothed, not by the arguments, which she never quite bought, but by his deep modulated tones and the trees. What a fake, she now thinks. What a big fucking fake her uncle is.

But all that does not matter any more. Whether Deepak is culpable or not does not matter any more. And Siddharth will probably turn out to be another garden-variety good Punjabi boy. She finishes her eleventh game of Capsule and sets her cellphone down. It is now time for the real games to begin, she thinks, which will start with a strategic decision on her look for the date. After some deliberation she picks out a camel-coloured turtleneck and a pair of slightly frayed red corduroys. She leaves her hair unbrushed and open, and with a light hand lines her eyes in brown kohl and dabs on a little nude lipstick and blush. Dressing up to dress down: a timeworn trick, but one that works nonetheless.

A surprisingly nice looking guy in a white shirt and flat-front khakis stands up and walks towards her as she enters the coffee bar. 'Ketaki?' he says.

'Yes. Siddharth?'

'I'm sorry, I Googled you and your picture came up.'

'A quick background check?'

'You look even nicer in person.' He smiles.

'Thank you,' she says.

He smiles again. 'Can I get you some coffee?'

'Yes, please. An espresso.'

Siddharth is taller than the average Indian male – close to six feet, she estimates – and has a lean, medium-built frame. A sportsman, she thinks. Not golf or cricket, but perhaps tennis or squash. Although he has a greying crop of curls, his face is young, bright with energy and hope – it could even be described as cheery, if she wanted to be unkind.

'So you lived in New York too,' he says.

'Yes.'

'A designer, correct?'

99

'Correct. You've done your homework,' she says, smiling.

'Yup. When did you come back?'

'January 2006. It's been just over two years.'

'What made you want to come back?'

'A number of unexciting reasons – work and so forth. Anyway, we know all about me, so let's move on to you.'

He laughs.

'You returned recently, right?' she says.

'Nine months ago,' Siddharth says. 'Do you like being back?'

'Yes, mostly. You?'

'I think so. The work seems pretty exciting, which is why I wanted to move back, but I guess it's a little soon for me to say.' He pulls his chair in and now leans forward. 'Would you ever consider moving back to New York?'

'No, not really. Though my dad lives there.'

'I know, I was told,' and he presents her with another smile, which she is quickly growing to like. 'He's with Citibank, correct?'

'Correct. He's been with them for over twenty-five years.'

'That's pretty amazing.'

'It is,' she says.

'Do you miss New York?'

'No, not really.'

'But you were there a while, right?'

'Almost ten years.'

'And no twang – I'm impressed. I was there for about seven years,' he says, the silver-grey speckles on his sideburns lighting up his whole face. 'So where did you go to school?'

'I was in Modern School. Modern School, Barakhamba Road.'

'I was in boarding school.'

'Where?' she says.

'The Doon School,' he says. 'Then where did you go to college?'

'In New York. College and grad school.'

'Okay,' he says. 'I finished school here, got a BTech in engineering, worked in Bombay for a while, and only then went to business school.'

'Stanford, right?'

'Yes.' His phone rings. 'I'm sorry, but I have to take this,' he says. 'It's my mother and she called earlier too.'

'No problem.'

'Ma, hi,' she hears him say. 'I'm sorry, I was driving... Really? That's wonderful. How long is she here for?... You must go... Ma, how often does she come?... Exactly... Don't worry, we'll be fine... Ma... Stop... Yes. Okay, I've got to go now... No, no problem... Sure. See you... Bye.' He puts the phone into his trouser pocket and looks up at Ketaki. 'I'm sorry about that.'

'That's okay. Everything all right?'

'Fine, just fine. My mother's best friend from college is visiting Delhi after years and they're planning a girly trip to Udaipur.'

'That sounds nice.'

'Yes, but she's all worried about how my father and I will cope for a whole week without her.'

Ketaki smiles.

'They make total babies out of us,' he says with a kind laugh. 'Anyway...'

'What is she like?'

'Who?'

'Your mum.'

'She knows about you – she just doesn't know we're meeting today,' he says. 'But she's a good woman. Caring, fun…'

'That's nice.' Will he ask her about her mother? Ketaki wonders. Well, of course not. He would have been told that Uma Khanna died when the girl was young – but not to worry, she died in an accident and so there are no hereditary health problems to be concerned about – and he knows better than to bring up that kind of shit on the first meeting.

'It's good to be back with them – my mother and father. And as they get older I want to be around them.'

'Of course.'

'I saw some of the posters you've designed,' Siddharth says. 'They're amazing. And your illustrations too. You're seriously talented.'

'Thank you.'

And so the conversation goes. For the next two hours there are easy exchanges about how they work and play, good-humoured arguments about Bollywood and books, and limited disclosures about their personal lives. They do as two people who want to like each other do: speak only as the other would want them to speak; hear only as they themselves want to hear. It is that special time in a relationship, the first light, in which exists a generosity of spirit that seldom endures.

It is evident not just to her and Siddharth, but possibly to all staff and patrons of the coffee bar that something is on. In the perpetual chatter, the stolen glances, the coy gestures, it is more than apparent that a warm tension is growing between them. When they get up to leave she feels the quiver of a hundred pairs of eyes upon her. Everyone sees the possibility, she thinks. Everyone wants a slice of this delectable possibility.

Siddharth walks her to her car. In a gesture that cannot really be called a kiss, his lips skim her cheek. He asks if he can call her again, to which she replies in the affirmative, briefly touches his hand, and drives off.

Mummy went for a walk and never came back. That is what she would have said to Siddharth if he had asked about her mother. That is all she remembers. Later, a few months later, as she sniffed around for details, she learned that her mother had gone for her morning walk to Lodhi Gardens and was hit by a speeding truck as she crossed Lodhi Road to return to the house. She died on the spot. Ketaki never saw the body and her last memory of her mother was from the night before the accident. She and her grandmother were playing cards late into the night when Uma walked in from a party. As soon as she entered, Ketaki's grandmother got up and went into her bedroom. Ketaki remembers this clearly. Her grandmother did not so much as say hello to her daughter. She just stood up and left. What happened to Nanima? Ketaki asked her mother as they got into bed. Oh, nothing, Uma said. Just like I sometimes get angry with you, Nanima sometimes gets angry with Masi and me. You know how mummies can get angry with their children, and she laughed and switched off the light.

That was the last time Ketaki saw her mother.

Indeed mummies can get angry, Ketaki thinks, as she allows a crazed Corolla driver to overtake her, particularly when one daughter's screwing another daughter's husband.

Ketaki and Adil walk the tight streets of Nizamuddin, tourists in their own country, strangers in their place of birth. Through alleyways selling music cassettes, VCDs, food, and hunger, they find their way to the kebab shop that sells Delhi's finest beef tikka.

She must rid herself of the fine restlessness that has developed since Siddharth and she parted three hours ago, and who better to help her with the task than Adil. What she experiences is that peculiar kind of agitation that does not overwhelm in any way; that merely loiters at the outer precincts of perception. Spawned by her uncertainty about Siddharth, about how he feels and what his intentions are, it also comes from being fully aware of the impossibility – the plain futility – of speculating the thoughts of another. So here she is with her dearest friend, in the February evening cold outside the kebab shop, standing in wait of a second round of tikka fresh off the grill.

'Are you going to let me off so cheap for your birthday treat?' Adil says.

'It's about the best treat I've got.'

'It's long overdue, but it beats Wasabi, doesn't it?'

'It does.'

'It must have been good to have your father here.'

'It was,' she says, setting her paper plate down on the counter.

'Are you done so quickly?'

'I'm quite full now.'

'A little phirni for dessert?' he asks.

'No, thank you. But take your time. I'm in no rush.'

He rests his elbow on her shoulder as he polishes off another plate of beef tikka.

'It's even more fucked up now,' she says, shifting away from him.

'What is?' he says, throwing his plate into the makeshift bin.

'Things at home.'

'Okay. Should we find somewhere quieter to talk?'

'Yes,' she says.

'Your place?'

She nods.

Wordlessly they drive to her flat through residual rush-hour traffic. She fixes them stiff whiskeys and they settle themselves on opposite ends of the sofa in the living room. Adil takes a sip of his drink and turns to face her.

'You have trouble with your brother, don't you?' she says.

'Not really.'

'You almost never talk about him and when you do there's always an edge to your tone.'

'Really?'

'Yes. You never talk that much about your father either.'

'Maybe,' Adil says. 'But anyway, you were telling me about things at home.'

She looks at him and smiles. 'It turns out that my mother and my uncle Deepak were having it on for god knows how many years.'

Only silence can follow a delivery such as this one; it is the only response capable of keeping the moment buoyant, and Adil lets it grow to a swell around them.

'My dad told me about it when he was here. I never had a clue. In all these years, I hadn't the slightest fucking clue about it,' she says. 'Family drama at its best.' She takes out a cigarette from its pack. 'Fit to be serialized for prime-time television.'

Adil lights her cigarette.

'My uncle's a fraud. I used to think that he was the wronged one and that my aunt was always too tough on him. Now I don't know what to think.'

'It must've been really hard on your aunt.'

'I don't know. She's impossible to understand. And my mother…' Ketaki takes a large gulp of her whiskey.

'Your father has obviously been through a lot too,' Adil says.

'He has. He's moved on, though, and good for him that he did,' she says, stubbing out her half-smoked cigarette. 'But clearly not my aunt. She's stuck in some hell.'

'It's good that he told you. It'll be easier for you to see where she's coming from.'

'That's what my dad said. But I still can't believe that I had no idea about this. I mean I vaguely knew that my aunt had issues with my mum, but not for a moment did I think it was because of something like this. This: your own sister fucking your husband.'

'You were a child,' Adil says.

'And then she's made to look after that sister's daughter.'

'I don't think she was made to do it. I think that's quite obvious.'

'And then she thinks that that very same sister's daughter might also be screwing around with her husband.' Ketaki takes out another cigarette and lights it. 'It's so messed up. I'm so messed up.'

'Ketaki?'

'Yes?'

'Stop.'

'I'm sorry.'

'No, don't be sorry. I can't imagine how difficult this is for you, but – '

'I'm thinking of talking to her.'

'That might be a good idea.'

'It probably isn't. I mean how does the past really matter when the future offers no possibility for change?'

'I guess I look at it a little differently,' Adil says, looking down at his glass. 'I feel things can change – most things can change.'

'So you think I should talk to her?'

'Maybe, as long as you know why you're doing it.'

'I don't really think it's going to help, but I just want her to know that I know about my mother and my uncle. And maybe I should also clarify that nothing was really ever on between my uncle and me.'

'Okay.'

'But I can't imagine what my mum was thinking,' she says with another swig of whiskey.

'It's hard to tell.'

'Especially when she's dead.'

'Especially when she's your parent.' Adil slides across the sofa to Ketaki and puts his arm around her.

'Why did you burn your dad's walking sticks?'

'Sorry?'

'Remember how you told me that after he died you burned them all?'

'I don't know. Maybe I wanted to be free of him.'

'What do you mean?'

'Just, you know, get rid of him completely. He always had me on a tight leash. My brother got away, but with me he controlled everything – my education, my career, my life.'

'It must've been hard.'

'It was,' Adil says. 'But I let him. I allowed him to control me. Feroz, on the other hand, stood his ground. My father sent him to the US for an MBA, but he got a degree in education instead – because that's what he wanted. Feroz did what he wanted to do, not what my father expected him to do.'

'And that's why you have problems with him?'

'Who?'

'Your brother,' she says.

'I don't know,' he says.

'I guess he knew how to handle your dad.'

'Yes. By doing only what he wanted. He never bothered about my parents.'

'But he's good with your mum, isn't he? He takes her on holidays every year.'

'He does.'

'Sibling issues,' she says, resting her head on his shoulder. 'I wouldn't know anything about them.'

'Lucky you,' Adil says.

'Maybe it's easier being the lonely only child.'

'Maybe.'

'Have you ever talked to your brother?'

'Not really,' he says.

'Maybe because you don't think it'll change anything?' she says.

'Maybe.'

8

All dressed up and in wait of Siddharth, who called her in the morning asking her out to dinner and offered to pick her up, she tries to complete the last of the nine book covers for the Australian publishers, but not even a scent of an idea will present itself to her. She attempts a long expedition into herself in search of one and when that comes to naught she takes an excursion through websites specially bookmarked to deal with such a freeze. This, too, yields nothing. She gets up from her chair and dawdles about before lying face up on top of her drawing board and looking at the dusty blades of the ceiling fan.

Deepak was at her studio every day once he retired from the newspaper company that he worked for all his life, and she wanted him around. It was not for ideas or inspiration that she needed him; it was for the comfort of his presence, a quiet and constant presence that pottered about the studio as she worked, that provided her with a steady supply of coffee, checked her bills, read the papers, gave her quick neck massages and reminded her about her posture, and brought her combs of bananas, rastali bananas – fruit of her putative childhood. Quite like what mothers do, she thinks. She makes her own coffee now, and checks her bills, and last week she downloaded a little program that alerts her to check her posture at thirty-minute intervals. But Deepak is no longer here – and she should be glad for it. Anyway, she thinks, it is not him that she misses. It is not him in particular that she wants. Like most people, all that she requires every so often is the company of another heat-generating body in the room. Even one certified as Siddharth Nanda would probably do. That, however, could only become a possibility if she got off the drawing board and answered the doorbell that has rung thrice now.

After dinner at a restaurant of her choosing, she invites Siddharth back to her flat. They settle down in the living room, face to face across the coffee table with just the right intensity of heat, light, and music around them. While she begins on her third whiskey of the evening, he sips Oolong tea; he does not drink when he drives, which is quite unusual for a good Punjabi boy.

'What's playing?' he asks.

'Sarah Vaughan. Are you okay with it?'

'It's great. Are you a big jazz fan?'

'I have a few favourites. You?'

'I enjoy it.'

'Okay.'

'As long as I'm not subjected to the obscure stuff.'

'Okay.'

Then there is nothing to say – but enough was said over coffee the day before and dinner this evening. Now it is time to do. She reckons that if he could, Siddharth would leap across the coffee table and pin her down to the floor. And it is not one-sided; she would quite readily take his clothes off and help him take off hers. The only glitch is that her uncle Prakash and Vijay Nanda appear at the window, sipping beers and watching them. Then the aunties materialize: Usha and Shireen take their places on the sofa, seated on either side of Siddharth.

'Are you sleepy?' Siddharth says. 'Please throw me out when you want to.'

'No, I'm a late sleeper. Are you tired?'

'Not at all. Could I take off my shoes?'

'Of course.'

'So, I hope you're going to show me your work some day.'

'There isn't much to show, but sure. My studio's right here on the terrace.'

'Are you up for showing me now?'

'No, not really. Some other day.'

'Okay, but I'm going to hold you to it.'

She needs another drink now. For a moment she considers the impression this might have on him, but quickly drops the thought. If he thinks she is a lush, he thinks she is a lush. So be it. 'I'm going to fix myself another drink,' she says. 'Can I make you some more tea?'

'No, thank you.'

She returns from the kitchen and switches the CD to Shirley Horn's velvet tunes.

'Have you ever been set up like this before?' Siddharth asks, once she has reassumed her position on the carpet.

'No,' she says with a generous gulp of whiskey. 'Have you?'

'Never. And that's probably why I'm acting so weird.'

'You're not.'

'Really?'

'Really.'

'It's just that I don't really know what to do,' he says.

'Well, I'm not expecting a date for the wedding fixed first thing tomorrow morning,' she says, 'if that's what you're worried about.'

He laughs. 'Well, that's very reassuring. Thank you.'

'You're welcome,' she says, smiling.

'Would it be all right if I joined you on the carpet?'

'Yes, that should be all right.' Is this it? she thinks. Is this the moment when she must choose between being the good girl who teases, who rejects all advances until rings have been ceremonially exchanged, and the one who welcomes him with open legs? But then must she choose at all?

Siddharth walks around the coffee table carefully and lowers himself down to the floor, not two feet away from her.

'Are you okay?' she says, watching him shift from one position to another.

'I'm always amazed at how people can sit cross-legged. Look at you.' He stretches his legs out now and leans back on his hands. 'Okay, that's better,' he says.

'Good,' she says. 'I thought you might've been nervous.'

'I think I might be. It feels like we're not alone – that people are watching us.'

She is hit by the idea that they think alike, but she contains her amazement. How long will it take her to realize that it is not such a wonder, that not a single thought we have can truly be called our own? Then again, how many times has she found herself with a man who actually shares her thoughts? 'Maybe that's how set-ups feel,' she says.

'I guess so. Anyway, I'm still glad we met.'

'Yes.'

'And I'm glad you agreed to see me again.'

'I'm glad you called again.'

And then, as if by magic, the ghosts in the room are gone and they are alone. They are alone and free to turn to each other, to look at each other directly, then to close their eyes and let themselves be led by their lips towards one another as the sounds of Shirley pour over them like warm water in some riverside ritual.

Once the exquisite games of rule and surrender are over, they loll about naked on the carpet. Lying on his stomach, Siddharth has propped himself up on his elbows. Ketaki is turned on her side towards him and draws little paisleys on his bare back with her finger.

'So, when your mother asks you about me you're going to tell her that I'm absolutely fantastic in bed, right?'

'Absolutely. Of course, she probably still looks upon me as her virgin sonny boy – even at thirty-six.'

'Oh, so you mean you're not one?' she says puckishly.

'You're a wicked woman, aren't you?' he says, giving her a small bite on the shoulder.

'Truly wicked.'

'Anyway, so now can I see your work?'

'Oh, so now that you've seen me naked you – '

'I suspect that there's more to you than this amazing body of yours.'

'I don't know,' she says, turning onto her back.

At eight the next morning she is roused from warm undercover dreams by a loud round pounding on the front door. As she brings herself to an upright position, fumbles for a sweater and her slippers in the darkened bedroom, and finds her way to the door, the pounding continues.

'Quickly, Baby,' Gopal Singh says, as soon as she opens the door.

'Why couldn't you ring the doorbell?'

'There's no electricity. Now come quickly.'

Through her sleep-tousled hair she considers for a moment Gopal Singh's face and what it must be like to wake up to this grim countenance, as his wife of forty-odd years is fated to do every single morning of her life. Has the woman grown to love his sullen eyes? Does her petticoat warm to the sight of those dark, dour lips? 'What's happened?' she says.

'Deepak Sahib,' he says.

'What about him?'

'Deepak Sahib's blood pressure has fallen.'

'Where is Masi?'

'Quickly, Baby.'

There is a mild commotion in her uncle's room when she arrives. As she stands outside the hall watching the nurse and Om Prakash fuss around the body and the bed, it occurs to her that in the fortnight since her father's trip, in the fortnight since she was told about her uncle and her mother, she has not visited Deepak even once. But what has she to fear by going in now? The chances of her crumpling with grief are pretty slim – the man is only to be pitied, not mourned. She enters the room.

In the blinding white light of the truth, Deepak is a new man who stirs new passions. Looking down upon him, her ears begin to burn with loathing. She can only love him or hate him, she thinks; she cannot swim in that lukewarm gulf of indifference.

'His blood pressure is coming back to normal,' Om Prakash says, as he massages Deepak's feet. 'Deepak Sahib really scared us. His blood pressure went down so much that he became white, absolutely white. I thought he was going to leave us today. But see Baby, this is all Baba's mercy.'

'Baba's mercy? Baba-shaba,' Sister Shiny, the nurse, says.

No longer does Ketaki yearn to seduce her uncle out of his deep slumber, help to bring him back to being. But she really does not need to. He is managing considerably well on his own. If every higher cognitive region of his brain has been conquered, all primal forces within him have rallied together to survive. And without the load of memory, the burdens of love and hate, it is an easy fight.

'Where is Masi?'

'Madam is in her room,' Om Prakash says.

'We have to call the doctor,' Sister Shiny says. 'He is better now, but we have to call the doctor. This type of blood pressure dropping is very dangerous.'

'Madam said we don't need to call the doctor,' Om Prakash says.

Madam can wish all she wants that her husband would just die and be done with it, Ketaki thinks, but Deepak Sood is here, alive, and in no hurry to go.

'Baby?'

'I'll speak to her,' Ketaki says.

Neera is seated on the little cushioned stool in front of her dressing table, staring blankly at herself in the mirror. Ketaki comes into the bedroom and stands behind her. 'We should call the doctor,' she says to her aunt's reflection.

'It is not necessary,' Neera says, picking up a hairbrush and pulling out the odd grey hair from it. 'He is stable now.'

'It can be dangerous.'

'It is not necessary.'

'His blood pressure plummeted,' Ketaki says. 'The nurse says it's dangerous.'

Neera sets the hairbrush down and looks straight up at Ketaki through the mirror. 'It doesn't concern you.'

'What?'

Neera stands up and walks towards her Godrej cupboard.

'You just want him dead, don't you?' Ketaki says, following her aunt.

'I think we should end this conversation right here.'

'You want him dead, don't you? Answer me.'

'I think you should leave.' Neera locks the cupboard.

'You can't stand him, can you? Why don't you just come out and say it?' Ketaki snatches the cupboard keys from Neera.

'Enough is enough. Leave here at once.'

'He was screwing your sister, wasn't he?' she says, moving closer to her aunt so that she can feel the wetness of Neera's breath on her chin.

'I don't know what you're talking about and I don't think you know what you're talking about.'

'We both know exactly what I'm talking about.'

Neera's response is trapped in the smouldering of her cheeks. 'Leave,' she says.

'I will leave, but not until we talk about this.'

'There is nothing to talk about.'

'Papa told me everything when he was here.'

'Your father?'

'Who else? Do you think Deepak Uncle told me?' Ketaki says with a dry laugh. 'Or wait, do you think Mummy returned from the dead to tell me?'

Neera sits down on the edge of the bed. 'So if you know everything, what do you want to talk about?'

'Is there anything you want to say to me?' Ketaki says, sitting down beside her aunt.

'No.'

'Are you sure?' she says in a softer voice. Out of the blue Ketaki desperately wants to hold her aunt's hand, cradle it in her own hands, then bring it close to her face and kiss it. But she knows better than to act upon such an impulse.

'I cannot believe Vikram told you.'

'I have the right to know.'

'He should not have. It doesn't concern – '

'It doesn't concern me?' Ketaki says, her pitch rising again. 'Is that what you think? My mother was fucking my uncle who was like a father to me, and you think that doesn't concern me? You're not the only one suffering here.'

'It's all in the past,' Neera says.

'Is it really? Look at you.'

'What?'

'Don't what me,' Ketaki says. 'Just look at yourself. At least Papa was able to forgive and move on.'

'It was easier for Vikram.'

'Easier? Why? Because his wife died soon after?'

'How dare you say that,' Neera says.

'You grudge Papa too. You can't bear the idea that he's been able to move on.'

'I hold no grudges against your father.'

'That's why Megan isn't even allowed to set foot in this house.'

'That is not true.'

'Really?' Ketaki says.

'I have to go to the market.'

'The market can wait.'

'What do you want? You don't think I forgave Uma and Deepak and got on with my life?' Neera says, standing up. 'Well, I have to go to the market now. And if you want to call the doctor, you call him.'

No, her aunt did not forgive them, Ketaki thinks, after Neera walks out of the room. She cannot forgive her sister or her husband. Their transgressions are her sustenance. She cultivates the suffering they caused her; watering it, feeding it, reaping its harvest. It is what keeps her alive.

•

'Do you know something?' Krishan says, the bare weight of his body still upon hers. 'This is the first time we have done it properly in your bedroom.'

'It's the first time we've got past the hallway without clothes being torn off,' she says, bending her knees a little as a signal to him to get off her.

'Yes,' he says, smiling, and rolls off to her side.

Krishan is here because she asked him to be here, and she asked him to be here not for kind words, cuddles, or other gestures of compassion, but to bang her brains out – to bang her brains out of her head, and everything else with it.

'How is your uncle?'

'The same,' she says, shifting onto her stomach. 'How are you?'

'Fine, yaar, fine. But too much pressure. First my daddy was pressurizing me to get married, and now my brother-in-law keeps on telling him that I should do an MBA. He says it is good for me. It is good to do higher studies, have a good education. Daddyji says when people see the MBA degree framed in my brother-in-law's office everyone gives him respect. He says our clients will also give us more respect. I don't know, man, I don't like studies, I like to work. But Daddyji won't listen.'

'You're in a tough spot.'

'It is okay, yaar,' he says. 'See, I am thinking I will do it by correspondence. I checked on the net. There are many correspondence institutes.'

'That sounds good.'

'Yes, this way everyone will be happy,' Krishan says, turning to face her.

'Good,' she says, sitting up. 'So, here's some news: I met someone.'

'Meaning?'

'I met a guy.'

'Really? Cool, man. What is his name?'

'Siddharth.'

'Siddharth,' Krishan repeats, nodding. 'Cool. So what kind of guy is he?'

'What do you mean, What kind of guy?'

'Yaar, I mean what is he? What does he do? Is he tall? Is he Punjabi? What sports does he play?'

'He works in finance, he's pretty tall. I don't know about the sports angle.'

'Wow, man,' Krishan says, 'finance plus tall. Cool.'

'He seems like a nice guy.'

'Good, good. How did you meet?'

'My aunt and uncle fixed us up.'

'Fixed us up – meaning?'

'You know, set us up, arranged for us to meet.'

He jumps up from the bed. 'You mean for marriage?'

'I don't know,' she says.

'What do you mean, I don't know?'

'Well, I don't know.'

'But if your family has arranged it, it must be for marriage.' He reaches for his underwear from the bottom of the bed and slips it on.

'It's a possibility,' she says, bringing the quilt up to her stomach.

'But then why did you call me?' he says.

'What do you mean? Don't I call you every now and then?'

He pulls on his jeans. 'Yes, but if you are with that boy, then you should not call me.'

'I'm not married to him.'

'Yes, but... Man, your type of people are very funny,' he says, shaking his head. 'I don't understand it. I mean your family has made you meet a boy and you say he is nice, and even then you are calling me and we are doing all this?'

'Oh, so if I just randomly met some fellow at a bar and we started seeing each other, then it would be fine to sleep with you, but because a couple of aunties and uncles are involved I shouldn't?'

'Yes,' he says, sitting down next to her.

'You make no sense.'

'When it is marriage stuff it is different.'

'But I'm not married to him – we're not even seeing each other,' she says, trying to rummage for her T-shirt in the bedclothes. 'We've made no decisions, no declarations – so what's the problem?'

'I don't know, yaar. It seems very funny.'

'Well, that's how it is.'

'Are his parents nice?' Krishan says. 'That is very important.'

'I haven't met them.'

'You have not met them?'

'No.'

'Man, what kind of arranged marriage is this?'

'The two of us met for coffee in Defence Colony.'

'Alone?'

'For fuck's sake, Krishan. You're happy to have a fuck-buddy, but a man and woman having coffee at Barista is unacceptable.'

'Yes.'

'What?'

'See, marriage is serious. It is not a game.'

'Okay, whatever.'

'Yes, whatever,' he says. 'We have different family backgrounds. We don't think the same about such things.'

She continues to lie in bed as he stands up again.

'And I don't think we are just fuck-buddies as you say.'

'Really? Then what are we?'

'I like you. I like how you think and how you are cool and I can always talk free with you. It's not only this thing I like,' he says, pointing at her half-naked body. 'I thought we were also friends.'

'Of course we're friends.'

'But we should stop this,' he says, taking his wallet from under the pillow and pushing it into the rear pocket of his jeans. 'I like you so I am telling you. This is not right.'

When Krishan says goodbye, he does not shake her hand as he usually does, but gives her a hug. He tells her he will always be her friend and promises that if she gets married he will provide her with a lifetime of free roofing services. What if she does not get married? He is out of the door before the question can break free from her mouth.

9

It is Saturday and an unconcealed February sun floods the studio this morning. With fair ease and without respite she works on a logo for a lingerie company based out of Brighton. Pickle Me Tink, that is what the company calls itself. She got the gig off one of the many freelance job sites she is on. Whether it is because she is good, or cheap, or good and cheap, she does not quite know, but she makes a tidy living from that phenomenon called outsourcing. The rent, the bills, day-to-day expenses are all somewhat effortlessly met by this modern marvel.

The dull buzz of the doorbell sounds twice before she is able to drag herself away from the computer. In her sweatshirt and pyjamas, she ambles out of the studio, onto the terrace, and into her flat.

'Good morning,' says a sweaty, smiling, unannounced Siddharth, as she opens the door.

'Hi,' she says, looking up at him, then down at her own unbathed, unkempt self.

'I didn't wake you up, did I?'

'Oh no, not at all,' she says, surprised – surprised not just at the sight of him, but also at the idea that she might actually be happy to have an unexpected visitor.

'Could I come in?'

'Yes, yes, of course, please,' she says, ushering him in.

'I'm sorry, I should've called first,' he says, coming through the door. 'I was at Siri Fort playing squash and I thought I'd drop by and surprise you.'

'You have surprised me – and pleasantly so.'

'Good.'

'Coffee?'

'Yes, please,' he says, following her into the kitchen. 'I hope you weren't in the middle of something.'

'No, not really. I was just in the studio trying to finish up something due at noon.'

'Then I should chug my coffee and leave.'

'That's okay, I'm almost done,' she says. 'I just need twenty minutes to wrap it up.'

'Of course, take your time. Would it be all right if I wait in the studio?'

'Sure.'

He stops at the door of the studio and looks in. 'This is really nice,' he says.

'Thanks, my uncle built it for me.'

'Your uncle Deepak?'

'Yes,' she says, and walks up to her computer.

'I heard he's not well.'

'I really need to finish up this work.'

'Sure, I'm sorry.'

While she makes a few last-minute colour adjustments to her design, she senses Siddharth shuffling around the studio, browsing the shelves, glancing through a hotchpotch of her sketches piled on the drawing board, riffling through museum catalogues and magazines. Aside from Deepak no one has been in here – not even Adil. She turns around to see that Siddharth has now positioned himself on the stool by the shelves and is leafing through her book on John James Audubon. 'You're not bored, are you?' she says.

'Not at all,' he says. 'I hope I'm not bothering you.'

'You know what? Screw it. I can finish this later.' She wheels her chair over to him.

'Are you sure?'

'It can wait,' she says. 'So, what do you want to do?'

'This guy is good,' he says, pointing at Audobon's rendering of the Carolina Parrot.

'A naturalist and a painter — and the story goes that he was almost as skilful with his paintbrush as he was with his flintlock rifle.'

Siddharth smiles and closes the book. 'Okay, what should we do now?' he says.

'I don't know. I'll need to bathe before we do whatever it is we plan to do.'

'What about looking at some of your work?' he says. 'You don't need to clean up for that.'

'You're a persistent one, aren't you?'

He grins. 'No pressure,' he says.

'What would you like to see?'

'What would you like to show me?'

What would she like to show him? she thinks, as she stands up and turns to the full-to-bursting rows upon rows of her paintings and drawings on the shelves. What of herself is she willing to divulge? This is still the beginning; that most tender phase when two people are on the verge of something that could lead to love. A single wrong disclosure will destroy everything in an instant. She pulls out an overstuffed folio of posters that she had done in her Brooklyn days, in her quiet, happy days with Lars.

She watches as Siddharth sets the folio down on the drawing board and studies each poster closely and silently. When at long last he completes the exercise, he collects the sheets together in a neat pile and slides them back into the folio. 'This stuff is strong,' he says. 'I don't know… tough, beautiful.' He puts his hand on hers. 'I knew it.'

'They're linocuts,' she says. 'With linocuts it isn't difficult to achieve that effect.'

'That stork-like one in grey and red, that was particularly beautiful.'

'It's a crane, the Sarus Crane.'

'Have you shown your work around?'

'Well, this poster was actually one of the winners at the Colorado biennial invitational.'

She is ready to get up now, to get the hell out of the studio, but he wants more. He wants to see all her work. Why not rinse her in cold water, pin her limbs down to a dissection pan, and cut her up instead? But she obliges him, hauling out her paintings and illustrations and posters one after another with increasing speed until he has taken in almost all of her.

'What's in those?' he says, pointing to the boxes arranged on the lower third of the shelving unit.

They contain her mother's work, the stuff her aunt sent across. Ketaki still does not want to open them, but in the present circumstances she would do practically anything to divert the focus away from herself. 'Those are my mum's paintings,' she says.

Siddharth looks at her searchingly.

'Would you like to see them?' she says.

'Would you be okay with that? We don't have to.'

'No, let's,' she says. This is the first mention of her dead mother in front of Siddharth, and she can feel a cumulus of unease rapidly gather above them. Thus far they were able to keep her mother out; now she has come and will probably stay a while, then go and come and go again. But maybe that is what all mummies do. Dead or alive, welcome or not, they hover about their babies.

'Your mother died when you were young,' he says, as she pulls out a carton at random and puts it on his lap.

'Yes, it was a long time ago,' she says.

'My mother told me you were just ten.'

'What else might she have told you?' Ketaki says.

'What do you mean?' he says, pushing the box off his lap. She knows she has knifed him. 'I'm sorry,' she says.

'It's okay, it must be hard,' he says, trying to smile. 'Maybe we should do something else.'

'No, it's fine.'

'Are you sure?' he says.

'Yes.' Now is as good a time as any, she thinks. 'Open it,' she says, standing behind him, and hands him a retractable paper knife.

He makes a clean, swift cut through the masking tape sealing the box. Reaching in, he brings out a parcel folded in newspaper. He turns back to look at Ketaki.

'Open it,' she says again.

With much ceremony he carefully unwraps the package to find a set of six small canvases, which he arranges in two rows on the drawing board in front of him. On display are a series of oils in Cadmium Scarlet and Indian Yellow and Gold Ochre that are almost incandescent in this clear winter light.

'These are stunning,' Siddharth says. 'Look at these women.'

Over his shoulder, Ketaki looks at the figures that only just resemble women, that look more like cats with mammoth breasts in vulgar Jack Vettriano poses.

'She uses the same reds as you,' he says, turning around again to look at Ketaki.

'They're brighter.'

'Your mother is really talented. Seriously.'

'She was.'

'It must be in the blood.'

It must be in the blood, she repeats soundlessly. It must be in the blood. The same red blood.

'Is something wrong?' he says.

'No, not at all,' she says, with a special pretend smile that most people buy.

'You know, I really think you should look after your own work the way you have with your mother's stuff,' he says, helping himself to another box.

But it was not Ketaki who organized her mother's work. It was not Ketaki who lovingly and meticulously sorted, packed, and labelled Uma Khanna's entire body of work. It was Ketaki's mother's lover – Ketaki's mother's sister's husband. He organized Uma's paintings and illustrations; he hoarded them, he hid them in boxes in the garage – in boxes that would be discovered by none other than the figure of Neera Sood in a fine tragic turn that would have made Aristotle gush.

'Have you ever thought about doing a show?' Siddharth says.

'A show?'

'You know, an exhibition of your mother's paintings.'

'No, not really.'

'We should think about it,' he says. 'In fact, maybe we should think about doing a joint thing – you know, you and your mother.'

We? she thinks. Have the two of them suddenly become a 'we' now? Then she looks at him, at a face aglow with enthusiasm. 'Let me think about it,' she says with a smile.

'I'll help you. My mum used to own an art gallery and my parents have a bunch of friends in the art world.'

'Okay,' she says. 'We'll see.'

He leaves a half hour later, not soon enough, and she lies down worn-out upon the charpoy on the terrace. How much do you tell? she asks no one in particular. How much should your lover – lover? – know? And why must he want to know so much and so quickly? And a show?

The chain of questioning is broken by another buzz of the doorbell. This time around it is Gopal Singh. 'Rajma chawal has been made for lunch,' he says. 'Come.'

But she is being too tough on Siddharth, she thinks as she bolts shut the terrace door. He likes her, he wants to discover her, and so he is building an approach road. Why look upon it as an incursion?

'So Keta, we were right, weren't we?' Prakash says from across the dining table. 'Siddharth is a fine young man, isn't he?'

'He's quite nice,' she says.

The Mehras have been invited for the beans and rice special at Neera and Deepak's, and Ketaki cannot believe her good luck. She was dreading a lone encounter with her aunt.

'It's a match made in heaven,' Usha says, 'just as I had predicted. Neera, don't you think they are perfect for each other?'

Neera smiles.

'Yes, and a little birdie told us that you and Siddharth have been meeting a lot,' Prakash says.

A little birdie, Ketaki thinks, little birdie Shireen Nanda. A Pied Bushchat, perhaps. *Chek chek chek.* What else does this little birdie know and what else does she tell?

'And to honour this beautiful meeting, I have specially sung and uploaded a beautiful old song,' Prakash says. 'Hemant Kumar's "Na tum humein jaano". Neera, do you remember?' he says, turning to his sister. 'From *Baat Ek Raat Ki*? 1962, I think.'

Neera smiles again.

'And remember how I would sing it when you and Deepak met?' Prakash sings: 'Na tum humein jaano, na hum tumhein jaanein, magar lagataa hai kuchh aisa, mera humdum mil gaya...'

'Beautiful,' says Usha.

'Neither you know me, nor I know you, but it feels like I've found my friend,' Prakash translates. 'Isn't that beautiful?'

'It is,' Ketaki says.

'Have you fixed the dates?'

'Daddy, please,' Usha says to her husband, squeezing his arm, 'let's not rush them – that's what I also told Shireen. And anyway, summer weddings are terrible. It's just so hot and humid. You can't even wear silks.'

'I'm not rushing anyone, I'm only asking,' he says. 'What does your papa think, Keta?'

'About what?' Ketaki says, trying to fight an emergent irritation towards Siddharth. What else has he shared with his mother that she then tittle-tattled to her little buddies? Has he told Mummy about the great blowjobs she gives?

'Look at her, look at her, she's feeling shy,' Prakash says, nudging Ketaki in the ribs.

'Sorry?' Ketaki says.

'Now now, Keta dear, don't pretend as if you don't know what we are talking about,' Usha says. 'What does your father think about this whole Siddharth thing?'

'I think he's left it up to me.'

'These NRI types, I tell you,' Usha says, simultaneously shaking her head and swallowing a legumes-induced burp. 'Your father has become a total American.'

When the Mehras leave, the two women retire to the study. Neera deposits herself on the sofa and switches on the television to watch a replay of the Australian Open men's semifinal match between Nadal and Tsonga; Ketaki sits down next to her.

Neera is in an uncommonly gabby mood this afternoon. She talks about Tsonga's brilliant performance against Nadal, about the day temperatures rising, about how she has not moved (read: taken a shit) this morning and must resume her nightly dose of Isabgol. She prattles on as if nothing happened; as if no tough words were traded between them, no tough discoveries made − as if they still lived in a time when Deepak and Uma were a safe secret.

'How is Deepak Uncle doing?' Ketaki says.

'He's fine,' Neera says. 'Dr Nath came over last evening and gave him a clean chit. He said everything's under control.'

'Good.'

'You're watching tennis with some interest,' Neera says.

'It looks like an interesting match,' Ketaki says.

'You only used to watch it because your uncle would force you to.'

'He never forced me.'

'Come on, you have never liked the game.'

'I don't mind it.'

'How you would fuss about going for your tennis lessons,' Neera muses. 'Do you remember?'

'I didn't like the coach.'

'Every afternoon there would be a long battle between

you and your uncle. In the end he always managed to convince you to go.'

'It was too hot,' Ketaki says, pulling at a loose thread on the sofa.

'Yes, and your uncle sat in that terrible heat while you had your lessons.' Neera puts her feet up on the coffee table.

'I remember.'

'Your mother played tennis.'

'I know.'

'She was one of the few ladies in India who wore those little skirts like Margaret Court and Billie Jean King.'

'Interesting.'

'Today they all do, but in those days it caused quite a scandal. A string of pearls and a little white skirt. Papaji was not very approving... all the men and all the ball boys gawking at her. But she didn't care about what people thought or said. That's how she always was. Would you like some tea?'

'No, thank you.'

'She was a very good player,' her aunt continues. 'She would win all the tournaments at the Gymkhana.'

'Good.'

'Your uncle hoped that you would follow in her footsteps.'

'Too bad that never happened,' Ketaki says, and picks up the newspaper.

'How is this Nanda boy?'

'Siddharth, you mean. He's fine.'

'You haven't said very much about him.'

'You haven't asked,' Ketaki says, blindly flipping through the paper. 'But if you really want to know, he's a nice guy.'

'A nice guy,' Neera repeats. 'That's neither here nor there.'

'What else do you expect me to say? I've only met him a few times.'

'I don't know, you don't seem very enthusiastic.'

'I've barely known him a week.'

'Still… there's a lot one can know about a person in a week.'

Really? Ketaki thinks.

'I knew. I knew in one day.'

Ketaki stays quiet; one word could crush this rare moment of candour.

'Would you like some tea?' Her aunt picks up the remote control and turns up the television volume.

'No,' Ketaki says, and takes the remote from her to decrease the volume. 'So you were saying…'

'I was asking if you'd like some tea. Prem Malhotra brought me some excellent tea from Colombo.'

'You said you knew. You knew in a day.'

'All I was saying is that one usually has a fairly good idea about a person within a few hours of being with him.'

'You were talking about yourself.'

'It's not important.'

'Tell me.'

'It doesn't concern you.'

'You were talking about Deepak Uncle, right? When you first met him?'

'Yes.'

'And?'

'And what? I knew in a day that I would say yes and marry him.'

'Okay.'

'He knew too, I think,' Neera says. 'Anyway, it's all in the past.'

In the past? Ketaki thinks. People are fools to think the present can be partitioned – protected – from the past. They ooze into each other, past and present, creating one indistinguishable bloody mess.

'My, look at him at the baseline,' her aunt says, turning her attention to the tennis match on the television.

Ketaki looks up at Jo-Wilfried Tsonga, the gorgeous, hulking Muhammad Ali look-alike, now playing a golden drop volley.

'Whatever one may say about Blacks,' Neera says, 'they are very good sportsmen.'

'Dhruv, Dhruv Jaitley, but you can call me DJ.'

'I'm Varun. Very nice to meet you.'

'Hey, I'm Aditya or Adi – whichever you prefer.'

Siddharth would like her to meet his friends, and so not one, not two, but three of his old school buddies have collected at the Delhi Golf Club. Smiling, she proffers her name and a hand to shake, and sits down across the table from them. Siddharth shares a few thumps, laughs, and hugs with his boys, then brings a chair for himself from the neighbouring table and sets it next to her. Chief guest is feeling more like chief interloper; she hopes the feeling will soon pass. Mercifully, the bearer arrives in short order with premium Scotch, carafes of soda, and kebabs.

They try. These three men, seated in a half-circle in front of her on the terrace outside the club's Pub, try to draw her out, chatting about the sorts of things they suppose she is interested in, but not before checking her out, butt, boobs, and all. Their backs against a moonlit eighteenth green with the Oberoi Hotel and an ancient domed tomb looming over it, they talk about how hot Sid was, how cool he was, how all the chicks wanted him, how all the parents loved him. Once she helps herself to the whiskey and lights up a cigarette – once she becomes one of them – they grow more loose-lipped. A few customary tales of youthful excesses are told, a little cussing and a little teasing begin. However, to her surprise and to their credit, the chatter is neither dull nor tasteless. She senses that there is something between these men that runs deeper than the backslapping and the badinage. It is love, she thinks, not of the filial or romantic varieties, but perhaps of a kind that only men share – a kind she can only hope to know.

In all fairness, she, too, tries to be just as sociable, and makes quite a success of it. She amazes herself in these situations; she amazes herself at her ability to morph into someone else, to become, at a moment's notice, the person that she is expected to be within a given set of social circumstances. Look at her now, collegiate and yappy – only the sweatshirt and the eyeshadow are missing.

Further stories of yore are shared as more drinks and snacks are brought to the table, but there is really nothing new that she learns of Siddharth. So she had no clue about the incredible arc of his urine or his love for Engelbert Humperdink (not the German composer) and other maestri of the easy listening genre, but that he is well-loved, well-balanced, and successful – such a fine young man – she already knows. (There is a lot you can know about a person in a week, her aunt said.) And she will bet on her life that anyone, anyone at all, who has met Siddharth would come up with a similar reading if asked about him. Does such unanimity make him uninteresting or enviable? In her own case, there would, without doubt, be no consensus on her character among the people who know her. She has been told she is a coward, and then she has been hailed fearless;

she has been called a bitch, a baby, an angel; kind, too kind, some have said; aggressive, depressive, a basket case, said others. Now does that make her more fascinating than Siddharth? Or just out-and-out fucked up?

She looks at Siddharth as he chats away happily, animatedly with his friends. Could there be something that he keeps buried then? Something that shames him, a blotch on his past, a tiny macula that he hides?

Just as the third round of drinks are being served, three women appear at the table, dressed in black and toting impossibly small clutch bags – each one of them.

'And these are the better halves,' Siddharth says, rising in their honour and introducing them to Ketaki.

'We're so sorry,' Ayesha, Adi's wife, says. 'Our Pilates class got a little long, and then there was just so much traffic.'

'We've been dying to meet you,' says Varun's wife Sonali.

'Everyone's curious about the person who's finally managed to hook our Sid,' Dhruv's – DJ's – wife Anjali adds.

'Well, this is her,' Siddharth says, sitting down and putting his arm around Ketaki. 'This is the mystery lady.'

Ketaki smiles as they look at her, as they give her the once-, twice-, thrice-over.

'Drinks?' Siddharth says.

Without really asking, she is told all about his friends' phenomenally successful careers. Ayesha has a degree in art history from the Courtauld Institute of Art and runs a leading art gallery, while her husband Adi, who got his PhD in public health from Johns Hopkins, heads a US-based philanthropic foundation in Delhi. Varun and DJ, both MBAs from Kellogg, worked in the US for some years before returning to India to start their own hedge fund. As for their wives (also armed with MBAs from top-ranking schools), Sonali has recently become a partner at a major consulting firm and Anjali is marketing chief for a multinational.

Or at least that is what she thinks she hears – a peanut shell distracted her during the second-half of the telling.

'Are you okay?' Siddharth whispers.

She nods and puts her hand on his.

'You guys,' says Anjali, 'we've only been talking about ourselves. Now we want to know about the mystery lady.'

'Ya,' says Ayesha, turning to Ketaki. 'Tell us about yourself.'

No, she thinks. Please. No.

'Which school did you go to?' Sonali begins.

'Modern.'

'Oh my god, so did I,' says Ayesha. 'I'm so glad to hang out with a Modernite. All these guys are Doscos and Welhamites.'

Ketaki smiles.

'So Modern Barakhamba or VV?'

'Barakhamba.'

'Which batch?'

'1997.'

'Shit, you're a baby. We all passed out in '89.'

Shit.

'Then where did you do college?'

'In the US.'

'Wow. Where?'

'New York.'

'New York? Cool. NYU?'

'No.'

'Then?'

'Pratt for my BFA, Columbia for an MFA.'

'What did you study?'

'A bit of everything – painting, digital media, a bit of photography.'

'Wow. So now what do you do?'

'Mostly design work – dull graphic design stuff to pay the bills.'

'Ayesha, don't believe her,' Siddharth says. 'Her design work is quite something, and her paintings... you've got to see them. But isn't it great that we finally have someone in our gang who's actually doing something truly creative?'

Our gang? She of scattered ambition and ability? Worthy of initiation into this fold? And would she even want to be? She might concede to clutching a tote, but toting a clutch?

'Real talent here,' he says, leaning in towards her and pressing her thigh. 'In fact, I'm trying to get her to do a show.'

10

Through the half-open door she sees Deepak's naked body held up on its side by Gopal Singh. She sees skin gone loose, skin creasing, and an otherwise well-shaped bottom beginning to dimple. The body is sponged down neck to toes by Om Prakash, then returned onto its back. A hand towel is hurriedly placed over his groin. Deadweight, she thinks. Deadweight.

Neera stands at the foot of the bed overlooking the morning ritual: the cleaning, the creaming, the powdering. She turns around, spots Ketaki standing in the hall, and pushes the door shut.

Ketaki remains outside the closed door for a moment before opening it again.

'Wait outside, he's being dressed,' her aunt says.

'It's nothing I haven't seen before.'

'I'm sure.'

Ketaki leaves the room, followed by Om Prakash.

'Baby, should we go to the temple?' he says.

'No.'

'Baby, you know what today's date is, no?'

'Yes.' It's the day her mother died. Deathday.

'Let's go then,' he says. 'Let's quickly go to the temple and come back in time for lunch.'

'No,' she says. 'No, thank you.'

'When you were a child you would force me to take you to the temple. Om Prakashji, please, please take me to the temple. You would run in to ring the bell and watch the pandit. But now,' he says, shaking his head, 'now god only knows what happened to you.'

'I know. I'm sorry,' she says, and barges back into her uncle's room.

Deepak is decent now, dressed and ready to receive visitors, and his wife sits dutifully beside him with the morning paper.

'The nurse played hooky again,' Neera says. 'Always playing hooky. Doesn't even have the courtesy to call.'

Ketaki walks up to her uncle's bed. She strokes his bare feet. Alarmed by the blue panic of veins around his ankles, she massages them. 'I think he's cold,' she says. 'He needs socks.'

'They're in the cupboard. Gopal Singh can put them on for him,' Neera says, without looking up.

'I can do it.' Ketaki fetches a pair of navy blue argyle socks and brings them to the bed. As she tries to pull the first sock over his toes Neera glowers at her over the newspaper. 'What?' she says to her aunt. 'What is it?'

'Hold the heel up.'

She does as she is told and with a fair bit of effort manages to get both socks on.

'Prakash Bhapa and Usha are coming for tea.'

'I'm going to the Okhla sanctuary,' Ketaki says.

'Oh my,' Neera says. 'It's been a while since you went there.'

'Almost a year. Last March, with Deepak Uncle.'

'With your Deepak Uncle, yes. You also did Pangot and Bharatpur and the Rann of Kutch with him.'

Ketaki goes to the window and looks out at the gulmohar tree.

'You went on so many birdwatching trips together, the two of you,' Neera says.

Uncertain of the direction in which this conversation is going, Ketaki does not respond.

'Have you counted?'

'What?'

'How many holidays the two of you have taken together.'

'You never wanted to come along,' Ketaki says.

'I wasn't welcome.'

'You were never into birds.'

'No, I wasn't,' Neera says. 'That was your mother.'

'Well, then...'

'That was your mother – your mother in her halter-tops and flares. She liked all that nature nonsense.'

Ketaki sits down cross-legged on the dhurrie by her aunt's chair and looks up at her aunt, at this woman wielding her brassy rectitude like a weapon. 'My mother?' she says. 'Just in case you forgot, today is the day that mother of mine died.'

'So you're taking Siddharth? Planning to make a birder out of him?'

'Did you hear what I said? It's Mummy's death anniversary today.'

'I know.'

'Do you miss Mummy?'

'Why are you asking me such a question?' Neera says.

'I don't know. Do you?'

'She was my sister.'

'And?'

'And what?' Neera puts the paper down.

Nothing, Ketaki thinks. Still cross-legged, she bends over, resting her forehead on her shins.

'Keta?' her aunt says, her tone suddenly gentler. 'Keta, are you all right?'

Worry not, Ketaki wants to say, I do not feel anything either. It may be the day my mummy died, but there is no mush, nothing melting, nothing that will well up into tears; only something hard, something calcified deep in my gut.

'Keta?' Neera says again, putting her hand on her niece's back.

Ketaki straightens herself. 'What?' she says.

'Nothing.'

'No, I'm not going with Siddharth. I'm going with Adil.'

'Adil? Why not Siddharth?'

'Why can't I go with Adil?'

'Of course you can.'

'So what's the problem?'

'Nothing at all.'

'I haven't seen Adil in a while and I want to spend a little time with him,' Ketaki says. 'What's wrong with that?'

'Nothing is wrong with that.'

'Then why did you ask why I was going with Adil rather than with Siddharth?'

'Well, I'm terribly sorry. It's your life and I will not say a word.'

'No, tell me. Tell me what you're thinking.'

'No, nothing,' Neera says, picking up the newspaper again. 'I just get the feeling that with Siddharth you're not… I don't know… Something is holding you back.'

'Something's holding me back?' Ketaki says. 'And what could that be?'

'I don't know. You tell me.'

Ketaki looks up at her aunt, who has now resumed reading the morning paper, then gets up from the floor. Before making her exit, she walks around Neera to her uncle. Deepak looks up at her wide-eyed as she kisses his forehead. She looks at Neera as she kisses him between the eyebrows again, and leaves.

Barefoot, she leads Adil through a jungle of ten-foot tall rushes towards the river. As the warm fetor of the Yamuna thickens, her pace begins to slow. She looks around, left and right, and when they come upon a small clearing, she suddenly stops. 'Over there,' she whispers, pointing to a pair of cranes barely fifty feet to her right.

'What are they?' Adil whispers back. 'They're gorgeous.'

'Sarus Cranes,' she says. 'They're almost never seen here.'

A spectacular display of pair-bonding is in progress. The female crane holds still, while the male sashays about her with outstretched wings. Now they move together, tall as men, their bare red heads thrown back, their long, dark bills pointed skywards. As they dance, leaping and bowing around each other, they sing, and for every call that one partner makes, the other offers two. The movements grow frenetic and the song reaches a crescendo when the couple engages in unison calling – a complex, coordinated musical exchange.

Before the performance has quite ended, Ketaki turns around and makes her way up the path from which they came.

'Hey, are you okay?' Adil calls out to her.

'I'm fine. Just a little tired. I'll see you at the car when you're done.'

He follows her through the grassy tangle up to the banyan tree under which the car is parked.

'Should we go home?' she says.

'I'm all right whichever way.'

'Do you want to walk around a little?'

'Sure,' Adil says.

They stroll up the Left Afflux Bund of the Okhla Bird Sanctuary, one of the capital's last remaining surprises, and find themselves a bench overlooking the Yamuna.

'You're not too bored, are you?' she says.

'Absolutely not,' Adil says. 'There's quiet here, not a soul in sight, there's a river, there's green everywhere – it's easy to forget that we're sitting slap-bang between Delhi and NOIDA.'

'Yes.'

'And how many birds we've seen...'

On the Central Asian Flyway, the sanctuary is an important staging post for migratory birds, and on any given winter day a birder can sight over one hundred and fifty different species. She and Adil, with binoculars and Salim Ali's bird book at hand, have spotted sixty-one kinds of birds in the span of an hour and a half.

'Nothing beats those cranes though,' Adil says. 'Never seen anything quite like that.'

'I've seen them several times in Bharatpur,' she says, 'but not here.'

'I've never been to Bharatpur. I arranged a trip there for one of my French clients some years ago and he's been coming back every winter ever since. A real birding enthusiast – you should meet him.'

'I went there a lot with my uncle. When my mum was alive the three of us would go.'

'So birding runs in the family,' Adil says.

'Maybe.'

'Well, the next time you're planning a trip count me in. I'm not big on birds, but those cranes... that was a phenomenal sight.'

'Sarus cranes mate for life,' she says, bending down and toying with a loose chip of wood on the ground. 'Once they form a pair they remain together forever. I remember reading some report where this guy Hayes studied some seventy pairs of cranes over thirteen years and found only twelve divorces.'

'We could learn a thing or two from them birds,' he says.

'In parts of Asia they're symbols of marital fidelity and love. They're worshipped.'

'They deserve to be.'

'And the male and female share in all domestic duties – feeding and caring for their young, protecting them... Of course, they're under threat.'

'Of course.'

She leans back and looks out at the shiftless murk that hovers just above the water. 'The guide at Bharatpur told us that when one mate dies, the other kills itself. It flies high up into the sky, then plunges to its death.'

'Sarus Cranes,' he says.

'Sarus Cranes,' she says. 'I remember two trips that my mum, uncle, and I took to Bharatpur. My dad and aunt weren't there. Three of us shared a room. Mummy, Deepak Uncle, and I. Odd, isn't it?'

Adil looks at her.

She takes his hand in hers; it stiffens in her hold. 'It's my mum's death anniversary today,' she says.

'I'm sorry, I didn't know.'

'That's okay. It doesn't matter. We don't really do anything. My dad calls, we talk a bit about this and that – but never about my mother – and that's that. No pujas and ceremonies and shit.' She gives his hand a squeeze. 'Do you do anything for your dad's death anniversary?'

'No, not really,' Adil says. 'I don't need an occasion to remember him.'

'So you think about him a lot?'

'I do,' he says.

'I never used to think about her that much,' she says. 'I mean I did occasionally, but it was different then.'

Up until a few months ago it was very different. She would remember her mother as a child remembers, in colourful little tableaux. Mummy and her on adjacent swings in the park. Mummy waterskiing in her red chiffon sari on Dal Lake. Mummy and Deepak Uncle and her tiptoeing after a stranded Bar-headed Goose here, right here, at the Okhla Bird Sanctuary.

'Things changed after your father told you about your uncle and her?'

'I think of her much more now.'

'Of course,' he says.

'But it's not like I'm longing for her. It's not a longing – it's a fixation. Now I have this strange kind of fixation, this strange, new fixation about her.'

'That's natural, I think.'

She stands up, walks a few steps in the direction of the river, then returns to the bench. But maybe the dead are more alive than we know, she thinks. Their own bodies burned to ash, they take up residence in ours. They live and eat through us, breathe through us, suck the very lifeblood out of us. 'Anyway, nice weather we're having…'

'Indeed.'

'Say something.'

'So what's that bird there?' Adil says, pointing to a small grey-brown bird scurrying past in front of them.

'An LBJ,' Ketaki says.

'What kind of BJ would that be?'

'A little BJ'

'I guess a little BJ is better than no BJ'

'It's a little brown job,' she says, giving him a light shove in the gut. 'Brown.'

'Little brown job,' he repeats slowly. 'Interesting.'

'Birders use it for small brown birds they can't identify.'

'Got it.'

Leaning against him, she watches as a knob of Common Teal toddles around the burgeoning hyacinth and into the water. She recalls Mr Ali on this species of dabbling ducks: 'swift on the wing and good for the table'.

'How about an early drink somewhere?' he says.

'No, I need to finish up some work.'

'All right, another time then.'

'Yes,' she says. 'You know, I wonder how I would've reacted if my mum was not with my uncle, but with some other random guy. Would I have felt so shitty about it? I mean could I just be jealous? Could it be that I don't really give a shit about whether she screwed around or not, but because it was Deepak Uncle in particular I'm losing my mind with jealousy?'

'I think it's more than just the fact of your uncle,' Adil says. 'I'm not saying that he isn't part of the reason why you're upset, but it probably also has to do with your father and your aunt and the fact that she's your mother.'

'I loved – I love – him, you know. I mean I've spent more time with him than anyone else – right from when I was a kid.' She straightens up. 'But what kind of love is it?' she says, posing the question directly to Adil.

'I'm not sure you can categorize love like that.'

She slips into a slouch again. 'I always thought it was an uncomplicated uncle–niece relationship,' she says. 'Actually, I never really thought about it at all. I mean who really thinks about relationships they're born into.'

'That's true.'

'But it was my ex-boyfriend Lars who put it into my head. He thought there was something strange between Deepak Uncle and me. But really, I don't think there was. I think Lars just couldn't understand us. He thought it was unhealthy that we'd speak long-distance every other day. He found it weird that we'd go on little holidays together when my uncle visited the US or I was in India. I guess it was a bit odd, but Lars just couldn't see that in many ways Deepak Uncle was the most important person in my life. For fuck's sake, Deepak Uncle loved me, looked out for me. And I loved him – I loved him a lot. It was as simple as that.' She puts her feet up on the bench.

'I think Lars may have been using him as a scapegoat,' she continues. 'We had problems in our relationship, Lars and I, and they had nothing to do with my uncle, but Lars was convinced it was because of him, and for a while I was convinced too. But really, I don't think it's like that.'

The river shimmies silver and gold as the sun sets, and the deepening twilight casts a Gaussian blur on everything in sight.

'I know I acted a little weird with him after the accident,' Ketaki says, 'but there's never really been anything sexual between us. I think I just couldn't bear the idea of losing him. Maybe I was just trying to... I don't know... fuck him back to life.'

Adil's cellphone rings. He swiftly silences it.

147

'But how could he have been sleeping with my mother? And how could he have lied to me for so long?' Again she sits upright and turns to Adil for an answer.

'He cheated on me,' she says. 'That's what it all amounts to. That's what matters. And my mother. My mother cheated on me too. The two of them betrayed us all – my dad, my aunt, me.'

Fires are being lit nearby as the evening chill grows. The river's ripe stench now mingles with the smell of smoke, stinging the insides of her nose.

'You know how people say that monogamy is not a natural state, blah blah blah? Well, I don't buy it. If it's not a natural state, then it should be developed, nurtured. I mean is, say, empathy a natural thing? No, it isn't really. We have to learn the art. It's the same thing. Call me a traditionalist, call me naïve, but I think that's how love should be. Monogamous.'

'I agree,' he says. 'But for some it can be difficult.'

'And so they cheat on their partners?'

'Maybe.'

'Have you ever been unfaithful?' she asks.

'Yes.'

'Really?'

'Yes,' he says. 'Once.'

'Me too,' she says. 'Maybe fidelity is only meant for the cranes.'

Siddharth now insists upon meeting her friends, and of the two she has – Krishan does not quite qualify – she opts for her old buddy Priya. Adil would not work. She has not even told him about Siddharth. She cannot; for the moment she cannot.

When Ketaki calls Priya to ask if she would like to meet

up with her and this guy she has just met, Priya pounces upon the idea. Beside herself with excitement, she suggests a double-date at an upmarket lounge bar in Greater Kailash that is her husband Rahul's current favourite. Ketaki is hardly delighted by the choice of venue, with its questionable door policy and 'Expat Night', when white people are not only fawned upon by the wait staff as they are every other day of the week, but also enjoy other special privileges by virtue of their paleness. She does not remonstrate, however. At the very least it is a bar, dim and loud enough to not have to keep conversations afloat.

Ketaki and Siddharth arrive on the dot of nine as planned, and are seated at a low table on the second floor of the multistorey nightspot. In a cosy huddle at one end of a velvet sectional sofa, they sip their drinks, now and then nuzzling each other. At this early hour of the night there are no large groups of revellers; only an assemblage of straight couples arranged at various dark nooks in a billow of folktronica. As Siddharth pours sweet schoolboy words into her ear, she watches the twosomes; she manwatches the men made men by the women they are with. On their own these men are bankers or techies or businessmen or lawyers, flourishing or otherwise, but with their women they are heroes. Studly or soft-soaping, they are heroes.

A half hour later Priya scurries in with a cache of apologies and excuses that she fires at them before so much as a single-syllable greeting can be made. Then Rahul appears a few minutes later with but one complaint about the parking problem outside. Once wife and husband are settled, Ketaki makes the necessary introductions.

'It's really nice to meet you,' Priya says to Siddharth across the table; then, as a murmured aside to Ketaki seated next to her: 'He's damn cute, ya. Why didn't you tell me?'

'I've heard a lot about you,' Siddharth says, which is a lie. All that Ketaki actually told him was that Priya was a really old friend from school.

'Only good things, I hope,' Priya says, elbowing Ketaki.

'Of course,' Siddharth says.

'So, what do you do?' Rahul says to Siddharth.

'Private equity,' he says.

Priya slides closer to Ketaki, while the men have their mantalk on the other side of the table. 'KK, ya, I'm damn pissed with you,' she whispers. 'You never told me about your uncle. When I told my ma-in-law I was meeting you she asked me about him. I said I didn't know anything and she was like, What kind of friends are you? So he's like got paralysis or something?'

'Coma. Deep coma.'

'Shit, ya. Really sorry to hear that. It must be damn difficult for your aunt.'

'How's the little pug?' Ketaki says.

'Poochie's fine. So naughty. Like a little two-year-old child. But listen, ya, if you like need anything, you call me, okay?'

'I will, thank you.'

'Listen, ya, your Siddharth is damn cute. You think it's serious?'

'I don't know. I like him, I like him a lot, but we barely know each other.'

Priya turns to the window. 'Uff, what's there to know?' she says, as she tilts her head and pouts at her reflection.

Ketaki kisses Priya on the shoulder and lights up a cigarette. Looking across at Siddharth, she feels a sudden and acute urge to bound over the table and stick her tongue in his mouth. Instead, she smiles at him, feels herself flush.

Happiness restricted to a silly grin, she thinks. The blood of lust stanched in a blush.

Siddharth senses something of her leer and responds with an impish moue. 'Another drink?' he asks her.

'No, thank you,' she says, trying to get her foot up his trouser leg from under the table.

'Rahul, ya, now enough talking shop,' Priya says. 'I want to talk to Siddharth too.'

Rahul pulls a Blackberry out of his pocket.

'Siddharth, you know KK and I are like chuddy-buddies,' Priya says, 'so if there's anything you want to know about her, you just have to ask me.'

'Will do,' Siddharth says.

'I'm sure you already know she's like this totally fantastic artist.'

'I've seen her work – amazing stuff.'

'Totally wow, no?'

'Yes. In fact, I'm trying to convince her to do a show.'

The muscles in Ketaki's neck tighten. She lights up another cigarette.

'KK, now don't be stupid and listen to others for a change.'

'You tell her,' Siddharth says, smiling. 'And I thought it would be great if it's a combined show of her and her mother's paintings.'

'Ya, KK, your mother was an artist too?'

'Apparently,' she says.

'This is a totally amazing idea.'

'Anyway, let's see what happens,' Ketaki says. 'Should we eat?'

'Uff, you're just a gone-case. You should – '

'I'm hungry too,' Siddharth says. 'Let's order.'

The waiter is summoned, appetizers are ordered, and Ketaki deftly guides the conversation away from herself, her work, her mother, towards a more inviting subject: Siddharth.

Priya laps him up. She asks all the right questions – what he does, what his father does, where he lives, which school he went to and which college, how many brothers and sisters he has, and so forth – and Siddharth responds with all the right answers. There are a few things that Ketaki learns. For instance, she did not know that he had a brother and a sister; he never told her, she never asked.

A woman in a black sweater and a pair of harem pants approaches Ketaki. Ketaki glances up. The woman's face, crimped and gathered below the nose, ravaged around the mouth, looks down at her and tries to smile. 'Ketaki, right? Remember me? We met in Sangla?'

It takes a couple of iterations for Ketaki to rise from the sofa, steady herself, respond. 'Yes,' she says. 'Of course. Malvika?'

'Almost,' the woman says. 'It's Mallika.'

'I'm sorry,' Ketaki says, resting her hand on Priya's shoulder for support.

'That's okay – it was close enough,' Mallika says. 'So how are you?'

'Good, thank you, and you?'

'Fine, fine. How's your uncle?'

The table falls silent,

'He's at home,' Ketaki says.

'Good. Good.'

Ketaki fumbles for her drink and takes a long swig of it.

'I knew he'd be fine,' Mallika says.

Taking another gulp Ketaki looks at the woman,

wondering what it must be like to kiss those knurled lips, to nibble on that fire-eaten ear. 'Could I get you a drink?' she says.

'No, I should be going,' Mallika says. 'It's good to see you. You take care.'

The rain does not fall in the steady rhythms of a winter downpour; it is flung to the ground. Lightning strikes not randomly, but like it is chasing the living and the dead. They make a run for her flat from his car. He follows her into the bathroom, and watches as she skins off her wet clothes and wipes herself down before doing the same.

Naked, they get into bed and lie like spoons under the quilt, her back to him, sharing the continuing sound-and-light spectacle outside from the dry darkness of her bedroom.

'That was a really nice evening,' Siddharth says, his mouth at the base of her neck. 'Priya's really fun.'

'Yes,' she says.

His fingers drift down her spine. 'Who was that other lady?'

'Sorry?'

'The lady who came over to the table to talk to you.'

'Someone I met last summer on a trip to the mountains.'

'What happened to your uncle?'

'Didn't your mother tell you?' she says, a sting in her tone.

His fingers freeze mid-spine then disappear off her back. 'She did,' he says. 'Since you didn't.'

'You never asked.'

'I was afraid to.'

'And one more thing,' she says, uncurling her body to end all contact with his, 'Priya and I may be friends, but there are some things we don't talk about and I'd like it to remain like that.'

'Please don't speak to me this way. And I honestly don't know what you're talking about.'

'You don't know what I'm talking about?' She turns onto her back.

'I don't,' he says. 'And maybe we shouldn't have this conversation right now.'

'Why not? For fuck's sake, the paintings, the show – '

'Don't yell, please.'

'I'm not.'

In a fresh spell of lightning the room flashes yellow. Siddharth sits up.

'Are you leaving?' she says.

'No. Do you want me to?'

'How could you tell her about the show? I mean, don't you know...' She feels around for her cigarettes on the bedside table.

'No, I don't know. I don't know anything about you, your life, your uncle – '

'My uncle?'

'I was told you both were very close and he had this terrible accident and... and it must be really tough on you.'

'Yes. So what else do you want to know?'

'Never mind. I don't think we can talk now,' he says.

'Don't leave.'

'I'm not,' he says, and lies down on his back again.

She rests her head on his chest. What can she tell him? she thinks. What can she say about herself, her life – her uncle? Granted, one small kept secret will keep two people eternally asunder, but sometimes the tiniest revelation can be a relationship's ultimate rupture. It is best not to say anything – not to talk at all and do instead what naked bodies do best.

She glides her hand up his right arm, massages his shoulder, and kisses him behind the ear. He remains still. Now, as she noses his armpit, she lets a single finger wander down his trunk. As it crosses his navel, he grasps her hand and brings it to his chest. She straddles him. Knees bent on either side, she sways just a little, left to right, left to right. But he does not rise. He does not lunge for the bottom that makes her proud. She dismounts.

'I'm sorry,' he says. 'I just can't.'

So the odds of sex are low. Body hard, dick soft, it is going to be a challenge. No matter, she will manage. She will try again in a little while. First, though, a cigarette. Propping herself up, she lights it and watches the rain being hurled at the windowpane. She and Krishan once did it in the rain; on the terrace, just behind the studio, almost in plain sight of Mr Chatterji.

Krishan.

After a few long drags, she looks down at Siddharth, who is peering up at her. Take him she will: She stubs out the cigarette, stretches, and slides down the bed towards his crotch.

11

Yellow roses and white gladioli have been arranged in pretty clusters around the drawing room. On the dining table the Royal Albert dinner set, given to Neera by her parents at the time of her wedding, is making one of its rare appearances. The Mappin & Webb cutlery – another trousseau item that has spent its near-forty years on exhibit in the china cabinet rather than be put to use – is also brought out, washed, wiped, and placed on the table by Thomas and Gopal Singh, who are dressed in their workday best in white shirts and matching trousers. Siddharth is coming to lunch.

Punctual as always, Siddharth arrives at noon with a bouquet of carnations for Neera that she graciously accepts and hands over to a spiffed-up Om Prakash, who, along with Gopal Singh and Thomas, stands at the end of the hall looking at the visitor with all too apparent curiosity. Once the ceremonial introductions are over, Ketaki pulls Siddharth towards herself to kiss him.

There is a stir among the posse of men in uniform.

Neera gives the couple a fleeting look. 'Shall we go into the drawing room now?' she says hurriedly.

Ketaki releases Siddharth from her grasp and they follow her aunt out of the hall.

'You have a very nice home,' Siddharth says, as he tries to collect himself. He sits down on the wing chair by the window.

'Ah, well, it's a home,' Neera says, 'but thank you.'

'You have some beautiful carpets.'

'They're very old. We got them at the time of our marriage. You know how it is... As youngsters you're so excited to set up a new home, and you spend all you earn on collecting beautiful things for your house. My husband and I were like that. Never mind that we would be borrowing a hundred rupees near the end of every month from my father, but every weekend, every weekend without fail, we would go out hunting for interesting bargains for the house.'

'That must have been fun.'

'Oh, yes, very much so,' she says, inspecting the dust on the lamp next to her. 'But then as you get older your priorities change.'

'Yes, I've seen that happen with my parents as well. Except for upholstery and a couple of paintings, nothing has really changed at our place in the last twenty years.'

'Masi, shouldn't we ask Siddharth if he'd like something to drink?' Ketaki says.

'I was just going to. The drinks have been laid out,' Neera says, pointing to an array of hard liquor, wines, and their respective glasses displayed on the fold-up bar. 'Please have a look at what you'd like and help yourself.'

'I'll have a nimbu soda, if that's okay,' Siddharth says.

'You don't drink?'

'Masi...' Ketaki says.

'I do, but if I have one now it'll ruin my day.'

'A shandy?'

'Masi, he wants a nimbu soda,' Ketaki says. 'I'll go tell Thomas.'

When she returns from the kitchen, Siddharth and her aunt are in rapt discussion about Tata Motors' budget-car, the Nano. Ketaki perches herself on the arm of Siddharth's chair and plays with his hair as they talk about the sociological impact of this new car for the masses. 'You know, Masi,' she says, 'Siddharth is encouraging me to do a show. He wangled me into showing him my work, and just loves it.'

'Her work is quite remarkable, I think,' he says, taking a sip of his drink.

Ketaki bends down and nuzzles his neck.

'Keta, I don't want to deprive you of sitting next to Siddharth,' Neera says, 'but that chair is not very sturdy.'

Ketaki remains on the arm of the chair for a few seconds before she sits down on the floor at Siddharth's feet. Leaning against his legs, she can feel them tauten. She glances up at him, then looks across the coffee table at her aunt with a sweeping smile. 'You know Masi, he even suggested that we display Mummy's paintings – in a joint show.'

'Mother and daughter have a lot of talent,' Neera says.

'They really do,' Siddharth says.

'You know that Ketaki's uncle – my husband – is responsible for nurturing it – nurturing both of them – mother and daughter.'

Siddharth smiles.

Ketaki is silent.

'Keta, you must have told Siddharth all about your uncle,' Neera says, adjusting the angle of the coffee-table book in front of her. 'In fact, shouldn't we introduce them?'

'Maybe later,' Ketaki says, now fiddling with Siddharth's shoelace.

'Later will be lunch,' her aunt says, rising from the sofa. 'Come, let's introduce them now.'

Siddharth looks down at Ketaki. 'Let's go,' he says.

She slides her bottom away from his feet to make room for him to get up.

'Shall we?' he says, as Neera stands at the door.

Ketaki shifts her weight onto her haunches, watches Neera and Siddharth leave the room, then slowly pushes herself off the floor.

'Deep? Deepak? See, you have a visitor,' Neera says, poised by her husband's bed. 'Keta's new friend Siddharth is here to meet you.'

Deepak looks up at the ceiling fan.

Siddharth stands at the foot of the bed, his head bowed slightly.

'Deep? Say hello to Siddharth.'

Siddharth mumbles a greeting.

Ketaki comes up to Siddharth from behind and puts her arms around his waist. 'So this is my uncle Deepak,' she says.

'Yes,' Siddharth says, and slinks out of her hold.

'Come and sit down, Siddharth,' Neera says, patting the vacant spot next to her on the sofa. 'Please make yourself at home.'

'It's more comfortable in the drawing room,' Ketaki says.

'Why don't we just sit here?' Neera says. 'Deepak Uncle is always delighted to have company, especially Keta's. Siddharth, you don't mind, do you?'

'No, of course not,' Siddharth says, taking a seat next to Neera.

Ketaki squeezes herself between Neera and Siddharth on the sofa. Siddharth stiffens as she takes his hand and places it on her thigh. Neera looks at her, then looks away towards her husband.

'As you must know, Siddharth, Keta and her uncle were very close,' Neera says.

Siddharth nods.

'Inseparable, you know. These two were inseparable. Every waking moment together. Isn't that so, Deep?' Neera says, turning to her husband.

Deep will not answer.

With a single knock on the door, Gopal Singh enters with a tray and places it on the trolley next to Deepak's bed.

'It's lunch time for Deepak,' Neera says with exaggerated cheer.

'Should we go to the drawing room?' Ketaki says.

'Siddharth, you don't have a problem sitting here, do you?' Neera says, putting her hand on his knee.

'No, not at all.'

'Good. I like being with my husband during mealtimes.'

Gopal Singh gingerly raises Deepak's head and slides two pillows behind it.

'You know, even when she was away in America,' Neera continues, 'Keta and her uncle would speak on the phone all the time.'

From under the sheet draped over the body, Gopal Singh brings out the feeding tube that disappears into the stomach. To this he attaches a syringe. He pulls back on the plunger and inspects the yellow-green guck that has been sucked out.

'In those days it cost something like a hundred or a hundred and fifty rupees a minute to call America,' Neera says, 'but that never stopped them.'

Gopal Singh now removes the syringe and attaches the tip of the feeding tube to the tube of the food container. He slowly opens the tube's clamp and a porridge-coloured liquid begins to chug through it: Lunch.

'Every night the two of them spoke. Every – '

'It wasn't every night,' Ketaki says.

'All right, maybe it was every alternate night,' her aunt says, lifting up a long strand of hair from the floor. 'But the two were close, very close.'

'I can imagine,' Siddharth says. 'This must be very difficult for you all.'

'Yes, yes it is,' Neera says. 'But such is life. One must take the good with the bad. Isn't it, Keta?'

'Yes,' she says, then turns to Siddharth and takes his earlobe in her mouth.

Neera stands up.

'What is it, Masi?' Ketaki says, retreating from Siddharth. 'Is something bothering you?'

Siddharth lowers his head and wipes his ear.

'Masi? Is something wrong?' she says, smiling up at her aunt.

Neera glances down at them. 'Nothing,' she says. 'Lunch?'

'Should we do some selections for the show?' she says to Siddharth as they return to her flat after lunch.

'Maybe in a while,' he says, walking towards the living room.

'Food coma?' she says, poking his bottom.

Siddharth sits uncharacteristically subdued on her mock Bertoia chair. She comes up to him, parts his legs, and sits between them on the carpet. 'Are you okay?' she says, staring up at him.

His eyes are closed. He says nothing.

'Hey, are you okay?'

He opens his eyes. 'I'm fine,' he says.

'That was a little weird, wasn't it? I'm sorry.'

'What was?'

'You know, my aunt dragging you to meet my uncle,' she says, resting her chin on his knee. 'Welcome to my family.'

He looks at her and runs the back of his hand down her cheek.

'What?' she says.

'Nothing.'

'What are you thinking?'

'Nothing really,' he says. 'I guess it's a little different with my family.'

'What do you mean?'

'I guess I wouldn't nibble at your ear in front of my parents.'

'I'm sorry.'

'It's okay. I guess we're more formal at home... not so demonstrative.'

She buries her face in his lap.

'Don't worry, it's nothing,' he says. 'Maybe my parents are just a little more traditional. Or I'm just a little uncomfortable with public displays of affection.'

'I'm sorry.'

He lifts her up onto his lap. 'Are you ready to meet them?'

'Your parents?' she says.

'Yes. I'd like you to meet them – and I think they'd really like to meet you too. You know, earlier I thought you may not be ready,' he says, 'and honestly, I was surprised when you invited me to your aunt and uncle's. But I'm glad I met them.'

She slouches forward, hiding her face in his neck.

'It must be really difficult for you all,' he says, stroking the back of her head. 'Look, I know you're not comfortable talking about it, but if you want to, or if you need anything, I just want you to know I'm around.'

She sits upright, her face only inches away from his. 'Yes,' she says. 'Thank you.'

He smiles and kisses her on the nose. 'So you were saying that we could start choosing the paintings?'

'Yes. And just so you know,' she says, fingering his shirt collar, 'I'll be happy to meet your parents.'

Not before a little groping and rolling around on the carpet, the two of them go into the studio.

Siddharth immediately takes charge. Curatorial from the outset, he devises a general conceptual approach that will guide their selection, with which she is in full agreement. They begin by choosing thirty of her works that she has done in the last five years – collages, posters, paintings, and some drawings. During the process Siddharth carefully documents each piece, whether chosen or not, and tries to sort out the mass of her work into chronological order. Once they complete the selection, which does not take very long as there is little difference of opinion in their choices, Siddharth decides that they will pick fifteen of her mother's paintings that bear some thematic or formal relationship to those of Ketaki's works they have already chosen. She is unconvinced that any connections can be forged between her work and her mother's. It seems forced to her, somewhat simplistic, but she does not object. Things are good; here is a gorgeous man who is so spirited about her work, so supportive – why spoil it all?

They crouch before the lower shelves on which her mother's boxes are stored.

'What's in this one?' Siddharth says, tapping a carton labelled 'BOX NO. 3'.

'I don't know,' she says.

'You really haven't opened many of these boxes, have you?'

'No.' She plays with her silver ring.

'It must be really difficult.'

'I don't know.'

'Should we not do this?' he says, looking at her.

'No, it's okay,' she says. 'Should we open this one then?'

Box number three holds seven small paintings of crows done by her mother. Each acrylic has a solitary crow set against a brilliant white background. The birds are painted in vigorous single tones: Perinone Orange, Cerulean Blue, Cadmium Scarlet. Again, there is a childlike quality to them, but the innocence is undermined in the immediate realization that the birds are dead, stuffed. Along with the canvases she finds several loose feathers in the box.

'This is going to be a lot easier than I thought,' Siddharth says, pulling out one of the collages Ketaki used for the Sydney publisher's project. 'Look at this.' He sets this down next to one of her mother's paintings. 'Look at the similarity. I mean besides the fact that you both have used crows, even the colours you use, the bold strokes…'

'Her stuff is more stylized,' Ketaki says, taking out one of the feathers from the box, possibly a flight feather from a kite, and beginning to tug at its barbs.

'Maybe. But the similarities are striking.'

'Maybe.'

They go on like this, with Siddharth making all too easy connections between mother and daughter, and Ketaki in quiescent agreement, until fifteen of Uma Khanna's paintings have been selected.

'This is just amazing,' he says, as he surveys the spread of artwork before him.

'You know what's really amazing?' she says. 'I didn't even really know my mother painted. I know she was this hotshot illustrator of books, but I had no clue about this.'

'Your father or your aunt never told you?'

'No. Maybe they didn't know about it either.'

'But... but then who put them all together?'

That deadweight you met at lunch, she wants to say but knows not to, and does not need to: she can see Siddharth nibble at his lower lip as he cooks up a more digestible answer than the one she might offer.

'I guess it's just one of those things,' he says at last. 'Your dad probably assumed you already knew and then didn't talk about it. This kind of thing is difficult to talk about.'

'Maybe.'

'But this just makes it all the more amazing – you haven't even seen your mother's work and still there are such striking similarities,' he says, standing up. 'It really must be in the blood.'

In the scented darkness of the terrace she lies sprawled on the charpoy waiting for Adil to arrive. She is tired from the day; tired of doing things she did not necessarily want to, saying things she would rather not have said. Even though she is older and better trained to capitulate, submission still is not easy.

Adil appears with a fine bottle of single malt. She hugs him hard; she is delighted to see both him and the booze.

She brings out tumblers to the terrace, he pours them drinks, and they sit face to face on opposite ends of the charpoy. After a little chatter about this and that, after the whiskey strikes, she sets her glass down. 'I've met someone,' she says.

'Congratulations,' he says. 'That's wonderful.'

Before proceeding further, she awaits any changes in the patterns on his face. There are none that she can detect. 'Thank you,' she says.

'And how's it going?'

'Quite well.' She lights up a cigarette. 'I invited him over to meet my aunt today.'

'You must be quite serious about him then.'

'Yes, seriously messed up.'

'Come on.'

Why did she call Siddharth over to her aunt's? she thinks. Was it really to seek her approval? To invite him to belong? Or was it something more twisted than that? 'I was all over him,' she says. 'And not necessarily because I wanted to.'

'What does that mean?'

'The three of us were standing in the hall and I kissed him smack on the mouth in front of my aunt, and then when we were all in my uncle's room I was nibbling on his ear.'

'Okay...'

'Maybe I did it to show her how desperately into him I am so that she doesn't suspect anything between my uncle and me. But she acted pretty strangely too.'

'What did she think of him?' Adil says.

'She went all out for him.'

'That's very nice of her.'

It was very nice of Neera. She really did pull out all stops for the occasion. But why? Did she have twisted aims too? Under normal circumstances, in the homes of happy, well-functioning families, such an extravaganza would hardly be surprising. After all, a prospective son-in-law, the man who could make a good woman out of the daughter of the house, is coming to lunch. But was her aunt's demonstration this afternoon – the flowers and the fine china and the extensive menu – actually born of a feeling of celebration?

'Is something troubling you?' Adil says.

'No, not really.'

'It's natural to feel a little scared by it all,' he says,

166

'especially when it feels so good. But it's better to feel scared than to feel nothing, isn't it?'

'Yes.'

'You do know I'd do anything to be in your shoes.'

'Really?'

'Absolutely.'

She leans back on her elbows and looks up to catch the tail-lights of a plane headed south towards the airport.

'Oy, you're beginning to brood,' Adil says, shaking her outstretched leg. 'So this lucky man goes by the name of...?'

'Siddharth.'

'Siddharth. And what does Siddharth do?'

'He's in private equity or something,' she says. 'And he wants me to do a show.'

'Sorry?'

'Siddharth wants me to put my work up – to do a show, in a gallery.'

'That's a good idea.'

'It is. I'd never thought about it earlier,' she says. 'And he wants to include some of my mother's work in it too.'

'Your mother's work?'

'Yes. I didn't know about it either.'

'That sounds very good,' Adil says.

'I don't know.'

'You don't know what?'

'I don't really know how I feel about it,' she says. 'I don't even know if her paintings are mine to display.'

'What do you mean?'

'They're not mine.'

'I'm sure your father wouldn't have a problem.'

'They're not his either, I don't think,' she says.

'Whose are they?'

'My uncle's.'

'Deepak?'

She nods. 'I don't think my dad even knows about them.'

'You haven't asked him?'

'No. My aunt just had them sent here without any explanation. All she said was that she was going through my uncle's stuff in the garage when she came across these boxes – boxes with all my mum's paintings and drawings.'

'Maybe you should talk to your father about it.'

'Let's see,' she says. 'And of course Siddharth knows nothing about my family, though I don't know... I don't know, my aunt was acting quite strangely today. Even if he doesn't know the details, I'm sure he knows that we're pretty fucked up.'

'It isn't that obvious,' he says playfully.

'Very funny.'

'Anyway, maybe you should consider talking to Siddharth. People are less judgemental than we think.'

This is true, she thinks. Just as people go on about human intolerance, it's pretty amazing to consider how much they are willing to endure of others. She is regularly struck by how K suffered her irascibility, J her capriciousness, L her insolence, and how A puts up with her foolishness. 'I know,' she says, prodding Adil's stomach with her toes. 'Case in point right here in front of me.'

He grabs her foot and squeezes it. 'Stop fretting,' he says. 'I know it's easier said than done, but why not try to enjoy it? Clearly he's a good man – for one, he seems very supportive – and you seem quite serious about him too.'

'So you think this whole thing is a good idea?' she says, studying him intently.

'I think so,' he says.

'You're right. I just need to stop worrying so much. And he's not a bad sort, really. He's warm, and he's caring, and I think he's generally fun to be around.'

'Well, then, there's little to moan about.'

'He's great in bed too,' she says.

'What the hell are you whining about then?' he says, slapping her thigh.

'But tell me, is this really the only way to be happy? With someone else? Isn't it possible to be happy on one's own, or in the company of friends — or family, if they're tolerable?'

'As much as I'd like to believe that, I don't actually think that's true.'

'So you're saying that happiness is only for those who are coupled?' she says. 'But you seem happy, you seem pretty sorted.'

'Sorted? Ha! And happy? I'm not miserable, but I wouldn't say I'm beside myself with happiness. I think I was better off when I wasn't alone.'

'I thought you might be put off with this whole business after your divorce.'

'I live in hope,' he says. 'I don't know. I may be a bit of a sap but the short point is that nothing means much to me if I can't share it with someone I love.' He stands up and paces around the terrace.

She knows that. She knows that well. Why is it that she and Deepak spoke on the phone almost every day when she lived away? It was this, just this: every unshared experience had to be transmitted for it to acquire meaning, for it to be truly enjoyed.

Adil comes back to the charpoy. 'You remember those cranes we saw?' he says.

Yes, she remembers those cranes they saw.

12

Siddharth guides her through a well-tended garden to the verandah of his parents' house. He slides open a glass door and calls out to them. Less than a minute later they appear.

From the word go she evokes all the right kinds of reactions from his parents. Very quickly they look upon her with deep welcome in their eyes. Siddharth can also sense their approval; he stands close to her, head cocked in her direction, luminous with the light of pride.

Siddharth's mother Shireen is a short lady, round about the hips, with a bright, pretty face and a lambent charm. Her husband, at least a foot taller than her – a beanpole – bears a remarkable resemblance to Alan Alda: generous forehead; poached, deep-set eyes; a thin but undeniably kind mouth. They betray no pretensions, husband and wife. Ketaki, then, likes them too, and almost instantly.

A keen gardener, Vijay takes Ketaki around to the back of the house and shows her the new fruit trees he has planted. She tells him of the variety of birds that they will draw. He is delighted by the information she shares – What a fund of knowledge! he says. Youngsters these days seem to have no interest in Mother Nature. He is delighted, perhaps, by her.

They return to the front verandah, where mother and son are sitting arm-in-arm on a wrought-iron swing and sipping their wine. It has grown dark, and Shireen suggests that they go inside.

They walk through a formal living area – the furniture is carefully selected without drawing any attention to itself – and into what looks like the study. Ketaki likes this place. It is not particularly large, and yet the house feels open, airy, light, even at eight in the evening. There are no susurrant corners, no shut doors, no walls that confine. Maybe she could live here.

She finds herself a spot on a love seat upholstered in dark brown hide. Siddharth sits next to her, while his parents make their way to button-backed tub chairs flanked on either side of the new couple.

'Siddharth tells us that you're a very gifted artist,' Shireen says, once they have made themselves comfortable.

'Not really,' she says. 'I do some graphic design work, that's all.'

'Ma, she's just downplaying herself as usual,' Siddharth says, giving Ketaki a light whack on the knee. 'You've got to see her work to believe it.'

'I hope I can see it soon,' his mother says. 'What kind of media do you work with?'

'I do a little in oils, some conté, a bit of collage and monotype.'

'I believe an exhibition is on the cards,' Vijay says.

'Let's see…'

'Of course it is,' Siddharth says.

'I'm sure Siddharth has told you that until a year ago Shireen owned a gallery,' his father says.

'He did.'

'And I'm sure she would be very happy to help,' Vijay says.

'I'm already working on it,' his wife says, winking at Ketaki.

'Thank you.'

'The pleasure's mine,' Shireen says. 'I believe you're planning to put up some of your mother's paintings too.'

Ketaki looks at Siddharth. 'Yes,' she says.

'That's a wonderful idea, a wonderful way to keep her memory alive,' Shireen says.

Ketaki endeavours a smile.

'You know, we used to see your mother play tennis at the Gymkhana,' Vijay says. 'What fantastic style she had! What an elegant backhand! She was obviously a lady of many talents.'

Ketaki attempts to smile again and picks up her wine glass.

'So I wonder if you know that your uncle Prakash and I go a long way,' he carries on.

'I believe you've been golfing partners for many years.'

'For many, many years. In fact, he was one of two witnesses at our wedding. If it wasn't for him we might not have been sitting here! Isn't that so, jaan?' he says, looking at his wife.

'That's true,' Shireen says.

'It's quite a story,' Siddharth says.

'It is, indeed. Shireen's father tried to hunt me down with a shotgun!'

Siddharth and his mother testify to this with happy nods.

'Our parents weren't happy that we were courting,' Vijay continues. 'Even though Partition was two decades earlier, it was still fresh in their minds. They had suffered – both families had suffered greatly – so they were very, very much against it. Since we couldn't get them to come around, we decided to elope, and Prakash was one of our witnesses.'

'True Bollywood style,' Siddharth says.

They laugh. Ketaki laughs too.

'Siddharth's mother wore a simple light green chiffon sari — '

'It was georgette,' Shireen says.

'Whatever it was, she looked beautiful,' Vijay says. 'Simple, elegant, beautiful.'

His wife colours like a brand-new bride. 'Okay, enough,' she says.

As they walk to the dining room at dinnertime Ketaki looks around. There is love here, she thinks, genuine love, genuine and functioning love that swirls about, spreads; is not stifled; does not settle in isolated nooks, stagnate, and die.

In Ketaki's honour, Siddharth's mother has especially prepared a regale of Hyderabadi dishes fit for those whose blood runs blue. Shireen asks Ketaki to sit next to her — I have to make sure you're eating enough! she says — while Siddharth and his father take their places on the opposite side of the oblong dining table. Shireen serves her. Large helpings of biryani and shikampuri kebabs and an array of accompaniments are piled high on her plate. Shireen watches her, smiles and strokes her back as Ketaki oohs and aahs over the food.

'You know, Ketaki, I also knew your uncle Deepak back in the day,' Vijay says, between mouthfuls, ' — and when I say back in the day I'm talking about almost fifty years ago. He was my junior at school — the Doon School.'

She nods her head.

'I'm sorry to hear that he's very unwell,' he says.

'He is,' she says, setting her fork down.

'Ketaki, would you like some more wine?' Shireen says.

'Yes, please.'

'School memories are so precious,' Vijay says. 'I still remember Cutty – that's what your uncle was called in school because he loved the mutton cutlets. I still remember how every single day he would sit down with one of the linen room bearers in our house – we were both in Jaipur House – and tell him all the news headlines and cricket scores because the poor johnny – I think his name was Tarachand – had inoperable cataracts in both eyes and couldn't read the paper. He was a good chap, Cutty... Haven't seen him now in years.' Vijay takes a sip of his wine. 'I really hope he feels better soon.'

'Vijay, darling, enough chit-chat,' his wife says. 'Let the girl eat.'

Siddharth glances across at Ketaki.

She picks up her fork again and drags its tines through a kebab.

'The food isn't too chilli for you, is it?' Shireen says.

'No, not at all,' she says. 'It's delicious.'

'Could I give you another kebab?'

'In a little while, thank you.' Ketaki looks up from her plate; Siddharth is still looking at her.

'Do you know the price of tomatoes these days?' Neera says, as Ketaki enters the study.

'No.'

Her aunt is seated at the roll-top desk checking monthly household accounts in a faux leather diary that has her name embossed in gold on the bottom right corner of the front cover. Such a diary is sent to her every year from her husband's old company, and every year when she receives it she complains to Deepak about how the gold lettering is so cheap and how you would think that after his thirty-plus years of service the least they could do is use real leather. So it is kept in the kitchen, brought to her at the end of each month for her to go through, then quickly removed again from her sight. 'Forty-five rupees a kilo,' she says.

'Stop buying them.'

Scowling at Ketaki from over her half-moons, she puts her pen down and rings for Gopal Singh. He comes in and promptly takes the diary away.

Neera gets up from the desk and comes to the sofa. 'How have you been?' she says.

'Fine.'

'You haven't come in a few days.'

Ketaki sits down on the floor at her aunt's feet and leans against her soft, heavy legs. There is certain comfort here in the lower folds of her aunt's sari. It is the same comfort that she got as a child, nestled in the silk, listening for its whispers. She rests her head on Neera's knees, and looks back and up at her. 'I had dinner with Siddharth's parents last night.'

'Good.'

'It was. It was really good. They're lovely people.'

'So I've been told.'

'His father knew Deepak Uncle in school.'

'Yes, Prakash Bhapa mentioned that,' Neera says. 'Anyway, I think I've found something that may be of interest to you for your show.'

'Don't you want to know how it went with Siddharth's parents?'

'You just said it went off very well.'

Ketaki sits up and turns around to face her aunt. 'Why don't you ever ask me about him?'

'Of course I do,' Neera says. 'But as I was saying, I think I've got something interesting for your show. I remember once going for this exhibition with Prem Malhotra at the Hungarian Cultural Centre. It was some kind of – what do they call it? – installation. It was something on Amrita Sher-Gil, and aside from her paintings there were photos and letters and other personal things of hers.'

'So?'

'Well, I found these pictures of your mother when she was young in one of Nanima's suitcases. You could use them for your exhibition.'

'I'm hungry,' Ketaki says. 'Can we have lunch?'

'Don't you want to see the pictures?'

'Maybe later. Could we eat?'

'It's not even twelve thirty,' Neera says. 'Come, let me show you.' She goes to her desk, pulls out a large manila envelope from a drawer, and returns to the sofa. 'Come, sit here. Let me show you.'

Ketaki does not move.

'You know I can't sit on the floor. Come, sit next to me.'

Ketaki complies grudgingly and seats herself next to Neera on the sofa. A dozen or so ageing photographs held together by a rusty paper clip are set down on the coffee table in front of her. She looks vacantly at her aunt.

'You don't want to see them?' Neera says, sliding off the paper clip. She picks up the first black and white photograph and sticks it in Ketaki's hand. 'Doesn't your mother look adorable in this one? She mustn't have been more than three. I remember this dress of hers – it was in a light lemony yellow. Ma had done the smocking on the front herself.'

Ketaki puts it down.

Neera flips through the pile and pulls out another picture. 'Look at this one with her tennis racket,' she says, leaning into Ketaki. 'Here she must have been ten or twelve. This was taken in Amritsar, at our house. Papaji had a tennis court built in the back. We had a Buick too. A burgundy-coloured Buick.' She sets the photograph aside and takes out another. 'Oh, you have to see this one, when your mother was in college,' she says. She puts the picture in Ketaki's lap. 'Look at the resemblance between the two of you!'

Ketaki looks down at a face that is hers.

'She was at Miranda House and my, she had all the Stephens' boys chasing her.' Neera takes her spectacles off and holds the picture at arm's length. 'I had a few boys chasing me too,' she says. 'But your mother, she was a very pretty girl.'

'And I look so much like her.'

'You do, don't you? And see this one!' Neera says, waving a close-up of Uma. 'The resemblance here is uncanny!'

Ketaki reaches for the envelope to put the photographs back. When she opens it she discovers another stack. She takes it out and thumbs through it slowly. 'Why didn't you show me this one?' she says, holding in her hand a picture of Neera and Uma, aged maybe twelve and ten, lying on their stomachs on a bed, big cheesy grins on their faces.

'I hadn't seen that one,' her aunt says.

'Oh really?' Now Ketaki finds a photograph of Neera and Deepak sitting on a lawn with a young and beaming Ketaki perched on her uncle's shoulders. 'What about this one?' she says.

'That's you,' her aunt says.

'I know.'

Neera fidgets with a coaster.

'And this?' Ketaki says, looking at a picture of Deepak feeding her ice cream.

'India Gate. Should we have lunch?'

Ketaki puts the photographs down on the coffee table. 'Happy times,' she says. 'It's interesting that you didn't want to show me these pictures.'

'I hadn't seen them.'

'Right.'

'Your father telephoned.'

'So?'

'He wanted to know about your mother's paintings. He said that you telephoned him to ask about them.'

'He knew nothing about the paintings,' Ketaki says.

'He knew nothing about the paintings,' Neera repeats. 'Actually he knows nothing about anything, your father.'

'You never told him about them.'

'What was there to tell?'

'Anyway, now he knows.'

Neera smiles a glacial smile. 'What does he know,' she says.

'And he forgives,' Ketaki says.

'Forgives?'

'Yes, he forgave Mummy and Deepak Uncle. He let it go and moved on.'

'It's easy to forgive when you haven't seen anything,' Neera says, her eyes glittering. 'If you haven't seen anything it's just a story.'

Ketaki picks up the newspaper from the coffee table.

'If he saw what I saw...' Neera says, snatching the paper from Ketaki. 'If your father saw what I saw – like those paintings. If your father saw Deepak weeping over them... He should have seen Deepak after your mother died, but he quickly ran back to Srinagar. He should have seen how Deepak cried. He should have seen how he sat in the garage for days on end with those silly paintings your mother gifted him. Deepak bought new boxes and naphthalene balls and cleaned and dusted and organized them. And cried – cried for days on end over them. Here, in my house, in front of me – I saw my husband cry over my sister,' Neera says. 'Your father didn't even know about those paintings.'

'Well, now he does,' Ketaki says.

'Your father didn't have to live with it. He didn't have to see them day in and day out going on like teenagers. He was never around. He worked long hours at the bank – '

'For fuck's sake, he had a job. What did you expect him to do?' Ketaki gets up from the sofa.

Neera grabs her hand. 'Where are you going?' she says, clutching at her, pulling her back down.

Ketaki is seated again.

'Then he was transferred to Srinagar. And your mother? Your mother refused to move with him. Used excuses like it was too cold for you or that Ma was unwell and she needed to take care of her. What rot.' She picks up the newspaper from the table, then slams it down.

'Ma was unwell. The osteoporosis, the diabetes – she was in a terrible way. And Uma asked her to move in so that she could look after her. But that was just an excuse not to go to Srinagar. Uma did not have a minute for her. She was too busy doing god knows what with Deepak. Under my nose. In my own house. And your father? Your father was in his little la-la land in Srinagar.'

Ketaki's eyes close.

'Are you listening to me?' Neera says, shaking Ketaki's thigh.

'Yes,' she says, her eyes coming open.

'And all along people were talking. Everyone was talking about it. Ma knew – your nanima knew. But your nanima couldn't say a word. Only watched. Only watched one daughter having an affair with the other daughter's husband.

She tried to console me. Ma would say, Don't worry Neeru, men are like this sometimes, he will come back. I made myself believe that. I made myself believe it was a passing phase. But a passing phase, my foot. A passing phase of almost ten years.

'I told your father only in – what? – 1987 or '88, but they'd been at it from at least '81. I remember. It was at our cousin Veena's wedding. Papaji was hosting the sangeet. We all travelled to Amritsar. You were – what? – two or three? I saw them. I saw them with my own two eyes. Right in Papaji's study, during the sangeet. In Papaji's study, can you imagine?' Neera pauses. In one swift move, she sweeps the photographs off the table.

Ketaki bends down to pick them up from the floor.

'Leave them there,' Neera says.

Ketaki freezes.

'But I thought it was a one-off thing. And I was wrong. How wrong I was. It carried on and on – for almost ten years. Late at night when he thought I was sleeping he would sneak out of the bedroom with the cordless and talk for hours on end with her. And Wednesdays and Fridays, when I played Bridge in the evening, I knew they went off on long drives.' Neera's body begins to rock forward and back. She grips the bottom cushion of the sofa.

'And I wasn't the only person who knew. People were talking. People saw them all over the countryside. Then at family get-togethers, you should have seen them at family get-togethers. All this giggling and laughing and silly behaviour in front of everyone. Teenagers. Can you imagine? Can you imagine how Nanima felt? They were shameless. Selfish and shameless.'

Ketaki looks up from her toes at her aunt.

'And with you, with you around it was even easier for

them. You were a great excuse for them. Oh, we're taking Keta to Sultanpur, oh, we're taking Keta to Bharatpur, and off you all would go.'

Ketaki's body slouches over to the side. Her head hits the armrest of the sofa.

'Keta?'

Her eyes close again.

'Keta?' Her aunt strokes her hair. 'But Keta, they loved you,' she says.

Ketaki cannot move.

'Keta?' Neera says, shaking her niece. 'Now get up. Get up,' She tries to pull her up by the shoulders.

Ketaki allows herself to be lifted, lets this sudden weight of herself now slump against her aunt.

'You're fine, Keta, aren't you?'

She nods.

'Good.' Neera sets her chin down on Ketaki head, then raises it again. 'But all this time,' she resumes, 'all this time your father was in his own little world – and treating your mother like a goddess. You should have seen him when I finally told him – I had to tell him. He had to know. How many more years could he be kept in the dark? But when I told him it was as if... I don't know. It was difficult for him.'

'You never confronted them?' Ketaki says, still drooped.

'Obviously not,' she says. 'And it was silly of your father to do that. Totally pointless. Did it change anything? Did it stop her? She still carried on.'

'And so did Deepak Uncle.'

'Yes, but your mother... you don't know what your mother was like. When she wanted something she made certain she got it no matter what. You don't know.'

'I don't want to know,' Ketaki says. 'Please, I don't want to know about – '

'No, but Keta, she was also special,' Neera says, the sting in her voice suddenly gone. 'She was really the pride of the family – of all of us. The pride and joy. Excelled in studies, excelled in sports, pretty, charming, ready to help anyone…' Neera's head nods to some hidden metronome. 'Then one fine morning she was gone. Dead. It was all gone, just like that. That poor girl. Just thirty-nine years old.'

Neera's eyes close. Ketaki rests her head against her aunt's chest, and the two stay quiet for a time. Then, slowly, Ketaki can feel the soft give of Neera's body grow hard.

'Yes, that girl could do anything,' Neera says. 'Play tennis, dance, draw, do ikebana, throw fabulous parties. Have children.' She now looks across the study at the window seemingly transfixed by the mosaic of rain dust on the glass pane or by the razzle-dazzle green of the neem tree outside. 'Although she took some time to conceive.'

'Can we stop now?' Ketaki says.

'You know, people would always say that you were the child he never had, but that isn't true,' she says, and pushes Ketaki off her chest.

Ketaki tries to sit up on her own.

'You weren't the child Deepak could not have,' Neera says. 'You were the woman he could not have – once Uma died.' She stands up and shuffles towards the window, her back to Ketaki. 'Or at least he tried to make you that woman. The art, the tennis, the birdwatching – Deepak was trying to make an Uma out of you.'

A rush of energy strikes Ketaki. She gets up and walks over to her aunt. 'What are you trying to say?' she says.

Neera is silent.

'Look at me,' Ketaki says.

Neera about-faces.

'What are you trying to tell me?'

Eyes glossy, she looks at Ketaki.

'What are you trying to tell me?' Ketaki yells.

'Don't talk to me like that,' Neera says.

'What the fuck are you trying to say? Tell me. Are you saying that he made me his lover? That I was his lover?'

'I don't know,' Neera says quietly. 'Whether he succeeded at making you her or you succeeded at becoming her, I don't know. I don't want to know.'

Summer

13

Under a wreath of incense Deepak Sood lies bathed and adorned on a bed of ice in the middle of the drawing room, his new widow seated on the floor by his side. Dressed in shades of cream, the couple are perfectly matched. Known and unknown persons shuffle in, paying their last respects to him, dry-eyed or through a run of tears. To Neera they variously nod, hug, or smile in condolence. From a little red box with a sticker saying 'Hindu iPod' pasted on its front, a tinny Gayatri Mantra is playing on loop at full volume. Sheila Seth brought it in as soon as she found out.

The air conditioner is on its highest setting, but it is May, and although only an hour has lapsed, the ice upon which the body rests is beginning to melt. Thomas and Gopal Singh have placed old towels and rags around it to contain the growing puddle, and Om Prakash has been sent to get more ice blocks; they need a supply that will see them through the day – only a six p.m. slot at the cremation ground could be arranged.

'I need a smoke,' Ketaki whispers to Adil, as they stand watching the spectacle from a corner of the room.

They walk through the house and out to the back garden.

'I'm sorry I got late,' he says, as he lights her cigarette. 'There was madness again at the toll gates.'

'That's okay. Thanks for coming.'

'No, not at all.'

She sits down and stretches her legs out on the grass. Leaning back, she looks up at an unseasonably dustless sky. Adil lowers himself next to her.

'Apparently, today's a good day to die,' she says.

'Sorry?'

'They were all booked up at the cremation ground. It was only with my uncle Prakash's contacts in the police that we managed to get a slot. It's at six. They will come to take him at five.' She crosses her legs and bends forward.

There is silence now. She can see Adil flounder. She can see him attempting a leap towards her and falling short. Death is divisive. Not only are you cut off from the person who has gone, but your grief also distances you from those still around. But is she grieving?

'Is there anything I can do?' he says.

'No, I don't think so. Prakash organized the obit for the papers, and he's called everyone, and he'll be bringing in food for the next few days – I forgot that the kitchen has to be closed until the fourth day.'

'Will your dad be coming?'

'Yes. Prakash called him. He booked the earliest flight he could get, but it only comes in around eight tomorrow evening.'

'Okay.'

'My aunt threw a shit-fit.'

'About what?'

'Because my dad's coming and she doesn't think it's necessary. There's nothing to be done, she says. What's happened has happened.' Ketaki pulls out a long weed from the ground.

'She probably just doesn't know how to react.'

'Maybe.' What is to become of Neera Sood, wife of late Shri Deepak Sood? Ketaki thinks. Is she better off now that he is dead, or has she now been left with a worse companion – loneliness?

'Does your dad need to be picked up?' Adil asks.

'The driver's here. I'll go with him.'

'I can take you.'

'That's okay,' she says, beginning to shred the weed. 'I don't even know what happened. Masi called me at four in the morning. Come. He's dead. That's all she said.'

Adil puts his hand on her knee.

'I wish I could cry.'

'Try.'

She smiles.

'You know how my mother's friend Bubbles Kochhar warned me against you,' Adil says. 'A girl of no tears, son. Don't ever say I didn't tell you. Cold, very cold, like all the women on her mother's side...' He leans over and kisses her shoulder. 'So if I haven't asked you to marry me, you know why.'

She smiles again. Maybe it is in the blood, she thinks, if the Mehra women have any. Isabel, her friend from graduate school, tearless Isabel had a genetic problem. She was born without tear ducts so that when she cried it was a dry pathetic yowl. But Ketaki and her aunt have no known lachrymal issues. What excuse do they have? 'We should go back inside,' she says.

The drawing room, which has assumed the part of an altar, holds more people now than it ever has in its thirty-five-year history. Ketaki wants to exit as soon as she enters, but her aunt looks searchingly at her. She sits down on the floor beside Neera and takes her hand into her own.

'Have you had some breakfast?' Neera says into her ear.

'I'm fine,' Ketaki says. 'Why don't you take a break?'

'I'm fine. Has Prakash Bhapa arranged for the transport?'

'Yes. An ambulance. It will be here at five.'

Ketaki looks down at her aunt's hand that rests in hers. She strokes it; it tenses for a moment, then yields.

Prem Malhotra, Neera's Scrabble partner, appears at the door larger than life in an embroidered white chiffon sari. As soon as she has Neera's attention she gives her chest a resounding thump and walks towards them with her arms open and her head shaking in simulated disbelief. She bends down and wraps herself around both aunt and niece in a single stifling embrace.

'Such a tragedy,' Mrs Malhotra says, releasing them, at long last, from her hold. 'Such a gentleman. Such a tragedy.'

Neera smiles at her weakly.

'Anyway, dear, you have to be strong,' she says, and hugs Neera again. She then turns to Ketaki: 'You must take good care of your masi.' With that, she slowly straightens her heavy self up and waddles out.

As Neera turns to her dead husband, her fingers curl into a fist. She tries to straighten her back, but in seconds she is stooped again. Without a minute's respite she has sat here cross-legged on the floor by Deepak for three hours now.

'Why don't you lie down for a bit?' Ketaki says. 'We have a long day ahead and you've been up since four.'

'I'm fine.'

Ketaki closes her eyes. Over the ceaseless whine of the Gayatri Mantra, there are whispers in the room about Deepak and T20 cricket and the terror attacks in Jaipur. When she opens her eyes, Adil is resting against the doorframe. Away from the guests that have gathered in a vulturine circle, away from the murmurs and the mantra and the dead, he is looking at her.

After several phone calls and some yelling on the part of Prakash, the ambulance – a white Maruti van with a detachable red siren light on its roof – arrives half an hour late. Two thin men carrying a stretcher made of bamboo are ushered into the drawing room by Gopal Singh. The pandit is brought in and commences with his prayer, while the women and other weaklings are shunted to the sidelines. Deepak Sood's body is lifted up from the ice and onto the stretcher. But for the chants emerging from the pandit and the Hindu iPod, the room is quiet.

Standing in a huddle by the door, Ketaki tries to support the weight of her aunt's body against her own as they watch four men lower themselves and slowly heave the stretcher onto their shoulders. Now the men rise, and along with the other silent onlookers, Ketaki and Neera follow the body out of the drawing room towards the main door. As soon as Deepak is carried out of the house, Neera lets out a wail and drops to the floor.

Ketaki steps away from her aunt and looks around helplessly. A wolf's howl has no echo, she thinks. Where did she read that?

Gopal Singh rushes to Neera. Soon a small crowd gathers. Water is brought, and sugar. But Neera Sood is out, limp-dead as her husband. She is hoisted up and taken in.

'Keta. Ketaki?'

Ketaki can hear someone say her name. She tries to bring herself back to this moment. There are thousands of people in the driveway. Prakash is in front of her. Adil stands next to her, holding her arm.

'Keta?' Prakash says.

'Yes?' she says.

'You go inside.'

You go inside. Her brain computes an instruction.

'Go inside, Keta. Stay with Masi. Adil, son, take her in.'

Adil guides her by the hand into the dining room, where her aunt sits partially revived at the table. He pulls out a chair for Ketaki.

'Thank you,' she says.

'I'll come by later,' he says.

'Where are you going?' she says, grabbing his hand.

'The funeral.'

'The funeral,' she repeats.

'I'll be back soon,' he says, gently freeing his hand from her grip.

Neera stares at them blankly. Adil walks around to give her a hug.

Ketaki stands up abruptly and the chair tips over with a loud thud. 'The funeral,' she says. 'I'm coming.'

Adil lifts up her chair. 'Stay, please,' he says. 'Stay here.'

She sits down again. He is rubbing her back now. She likes it. She looks up at him. He smiles. 'I'll be back in a while,' he says, and leaves.

Ketaki and Neera are left to themselves and each other. Thomas is next door in the kitchen ready to serve them anything, save what they want.

One by one, Ketaki's senses slowly begin to reawaken. The incense that still burns in the drawing room – and must continue to burn, the pandit commanded – snakes its way to her nose. The mantra loop grates her ear. She gets up, the chair tips over again, and Thomas rushes in.

'What happened?' he asks. 'Do you need something?'

Eyes glazed, Neera looks up at him, then at Ketaki.

'No. It's that mantra machine,' Ketaki says, walking into the drawing room.

Thomas follows her.

She yanks the plug out of the socket.

'Thank you,' Thomas says. 'It was giving me a headache too.'

She smiles.

They walk back towards the dining room.

Neera attempts to stand up, falters, sits down again.

'What is it, Masi?'

Neera's body collapses forward.

Ketaki rushes to her aunt to hold her up. 'Masi? Would you like to lie down?' she says.

'Should we give her some tea?' Thomas says.

'Masi, would you like some tea?'

She peers up at Ketaki.

'What is it?'

Neera rests her head against Ketaki's chest.

Ketaki manages to put a few spoonfuls of tea into her aunt's mouth. Into her own she cannot; her stomach convulses even at the thought of it. She sets the cup down. 'Masi, we're going to lie down now,' she says, trying to lift Neera up from the shoulders.

Too tired now to protest, Neera stands up and follows Ketaki into the bedroom. She asks that the lights be kept on and lies down. Her eyes are riveted to the bathroom door, then slowly they close and she begins to sough. Ketaki sits at the edge of the bed watching Neera, waiting for sleep to arrive and play its part because she no longer can play her own.

And soon it comes. The moaning softens into a susurrus, Neera's breathing steadies. Just to make sure, Ketaki lightly blows on her face. Nothing. She walks around to the other side of the bed and curls up next to her aunt.

A single pigeon has entered the arrivals terminal of Indira Gandhi International Airport without the fifty-rupee ticket, the smiles, or the wiles demanded of everyone else. It flies high above the millions in the building, circling them. Exhausted now, or maybe bored or frightened, it wants out, but cannot remember how it came in. The bird flaps its way to a large window, slams into the pane, scrambles against the glass, and flies away, only to return seconds later to the same fate. Over and over again: flight, collision, flight; flight, collision, flight.

Ketaki looks away and tries to direct her attention to the arrivals monitor that has not been updated even once in the hour that she has been here. She submits to the teaser at the Nescafé booth, and just as she is about to take her first sip of a tasteless milk and water brew, Vikram Khanna comes into view with his laptop bag and suiter. She puts down the paper cup on the counter and makes her way to a small clearing among the waiting crowds in the hope that her father will see her. Looking this way and that, he walks in her general direction. As she moves towards him, rubbing past a hundred people she does not know, Vikram stops, pivots left, and heads for a clutch of liveried men, each sporting a white chauffeur cap and holding up a placard in his gloved hands. She follows him. When she is just behind her father, within audible distance of him, she stops. 'Papa,' she says.

He turns around. In a few seconds a face grey with weariness lights up. 'Ketaki,' he says, and brings his arms around her. 'My Ketaki, my Sweetaki.'

Head against his chest, she closes her eyes as he strokes her hair. Vikram lifts her face up with his hand. 'Why did you come, darling? I arranged for a car. You look so tired.'

'It's okay.'

'Is Om Prakash here with you?'

'Yes.'

'All right, let me send the chauffeur off,' Vikram says. 'And thank you for coming.'

Om Prakash rushes up to them as they walk out of the terminal building. 'Sahibji!' he says. 'Oh, Sahibji!' He bends down to touch Vikram's feet.

Vikram tries to deflect this and pulls Om Prakash up from his shoulders. 'You're looking good,' he says, giving him a hug.

'Thank you, Sahibji, thank you,' Om Prakash says, taking the suiter from him.

'Should we go?'

They follow Om Prakash to the car. Vikram sits behind him; Ketaki lifts the armrest in the middle of the backseat and slides up next to her father. He puts his arm around her.

'It's been a difficult time for you,' he says, after some quiet minutes.

'Yes.'

'For Neera too.'

'Yes.'

'But at least Deepak did not have to suffer too much.'

She likes the cool, dark quiet of the car, she likes her father next to her in this quiet. Why the need to talk? she thinks.

Vikram kisses her forehead and turns towards the window.

She smiles to herself. So this is the wonder that is family: wordless communication, mind-reading. Her head against her father's shoulder and eyes closed, she is silently held in this wonder until they reach home.

•

Neera is not in sight, but Gopal Singh is there to play host. He receives them at the door and directs them into the drawing room, which has now reverted to its customary state. Tea and biscuits are served, and Vikram's luggage is put into the spare bedroom.

'Where is Masi?' Ketaki asks Gopal Singh.

'She is in her room,' he replies.

'She must be sleeping,' Vikram says. 'Let's not wake her up.'

'It's not even eleven. She never sleeps before midnight,' Ketaki says. 'I'll see what she's doing.'

Ketaki opens the door to Neera's bedroom. The bed is empty and unmade, and the sound of trickling water comes in from the bathroom. Her aunt shambles out, still wearing her cream-coloured sari from the day before.

'Papa's here,' Ketaki says.

Neera smoothes down her bob, tucks her hair behind her ears, and walks out. Ketaki turns off the running tap in the bathroom and follows her out. As soon as they enter, Vikram rises from the sofa. He walks up to Neera and hugs her. For her part she stands still, paralysed, hands by her side.

'Neera,' he says, 'Neera, I'm so sorry.'

She looks up at him. 'You know what it's like,' she says.

Like a child she lets him lead her by the hand to the sofa. Like a child she sits quietly beside him. Ketaki sits across from them on the floor, reclining against a brass chest.

'I told everyone to go,' Neera says. 'They were all just sitting here. But it's no use – it's a waste of everyone's time. And one needs time alone.'

'Yes,' Vikram says softly. 'And you need rest. You need to sleep.'

'We're going to Haridwar in the morning.' She glances at Ketaki, then looks down at her knees. 'With the ashes,' she says.

'Yes. Prakash Bhapa mentioned that to me. I told him I would go with you.'

'I'm going as well,' Ketaki says.

'That would be nice,' Vikram says.

'But there will be no chautha, no prayer meetings,' Neera says. 'Only this.'

'Whatever you're comfortable with,' Vikram says.

'We have to pick up the ashes from the cremation ground at seven,' Ketaki says. 'Prakash Mama's arranged for it with his police contacts.'

'That's fine,' Vikram says. 'For now I think we should call it a night. We have an early start tomorrow.'

Lodhi Cremation Ground: preferred venue for the who's who of Delhi to burn their dead. It is her first visit. In her twenty-nine years she has not attended a funeral even once. When her mother died, she was ten; too young to understand, everyone thought, much less to witness her mother aflame. Deepak stayed home with her that afternoon. He played *Jungle Book* on the VCR to distract her, but what actually riveted her was him, a grown-up man, an uncle, sitting on the sofa and crying like a little girl.

She would like to have been here yesterday. They say that the cremation ceremony helps bring closure. She is not entirely convinced that watching a body smoulder can really do that, but right now she would be willing to try anything.

As instructed by Prakash, they arrive at the cremation ground with milk, a cloth bag, a gunnysack, and a slip of paper to give to the pandit. The SHO from the Hazrat Nizamuddin police station is at the gate to receive them. He has been deployed here, courtesy Prakash, to ensure that the process runs smoothly. Neera, Vikram, and Ketaki get out of the car and follow the cop into a tiny room in which a tiny man dressed in a freshly starched white kurta-pyjama sits behind a steel table. He looks up at them and Vikram steps forward.

'We have come for the ashes,' Vikram says quietly, his head bowed.

'Sirji,' the man says, 'if you have to say it in English, say last remains. This ashes-pashes word is very disrespectful.'

'I'm sorry – last remains. We have come for the last remains.'

'Good, good,' he says, smiling. 'Number?'

Vikram looks at him blankly, then turns to the policeman. The SHO points to the slip of paper in Vikram's left hand. He places it on the table.

'Good, very good. We are ready then,' the man says, rising from his chair. 'But Sirji, before we proceed, would you like to give a donation?' He pushes a small padlocked chest across the table towards Vikram.

The cop steps in. 'Panditji, they already made their donations yesterday. Please, let us proceed, they have a lot to do today.'

'Sirji, I was only asking,' he says. 'You know what work is done here. If you would like to give something, give it; if you don't, that is also fine.'

They are taken to a yard at the back of the grounds, to a line of cremation pits that resemble shallow stepwells. This is where it happens, she thinks. This is where the body is set on fire. This is where a loved one will set the body on fire, then crack open its burning skull with a bamboo pole. The pandit points to the pit in front of them and bows before it. He begins a loud gravelly mantra recitation and gestures to Vikram to come down the steps to the pit. Vikram rolls up his trousers and descends.

'Now we will pick the flowers,' the pandit says – a euphemism, if there ever was one, for sifting out bones from a mountain of ash. He begins raking through the debris with his bare hands. 'Be careful, it's still hot,' he says, and points to Vikram to follow suit.

Ketaki turns away, to her left, only to be presented with the smoking residues of another cremation. She looks right and sees her aunt standing alone, clasping her handbag, staring directly back at her. The dull throb in the head that Ketaki woke up with is intensifying; at this point, she does not just feel the thudding, she can hear it too, hear it gain speed and strength. The pounding spreads: now it is in the chest, now in the stomach, now the feet. She should set herself down exactly where she is at, she thinks, lest her body pull a stunt on her and cause panic among the others. Leaning against a pillar, she slowly bends her knees and lowers herself to the ground.

It seems as if she has only just sat down when she is being lifted. She looks up. Her father and the SHO are crouched over, trying to raise her from the shoulders.

'You're all right, darling, aren't you?' Vikram says.

'Yes,' she says. She is on her feet again, quite steady now, quite ready to go on with the day's business.

'Would you like to sit in the car? Om Prakash is there.'

'No, Papa,' she says.

He returns to the pit. The ceremony is coming to an end. The time has come to wash the flowers. Milk and water are brought to Vikram and he pours them over the gathered bones.

•

They are in the car now: Om Prakash is driving and Vikram is seated next to him; the women are in the back with a sackful of ash and a bag of bones, which, not forty-eight hours ago, were a man whom Ketaki might have loved. Love, she thinks – no matter what kind – the experience of love is always short; it is the forgetting that takes forever. And in the end it is all the same. Whether he walks out on you, or he dies, or you cheat on him and leave, in the end this he, this flesh-and-blood being whom you once could taste and smell and touch, is gone, and all that you are left with are artefacts: a picture, a bauble, a bone.

The drive to Haridwar is uneventful. There are no overturned trucks, no processions, no road diversions to delay the mourners on their journey. The drive is also a quiet one. Neera manages about seven words that have mostly to do with urgent bodily demands – a request for water, a need to use the bathroom – and Ketaki, too, says little, as she tries over and over again to practise a meditation technique she was taught by a yoga teacher last year.

As they cross Cheetal, Om Prakash breaks into conversation. 'Tell me, Sahibji,' he says, turning to Vikram, 'when England and Australia play their big match, whose ashes are in the trophy? When they were playing last year in January, Gopal Singh told me that the trophy has ashes in them. But whose ashes are in it?'

'That's what they say, but they're not the ashes of a person. They are apparently the ashes of a burnt cricket stump or bail.'

'But, Sahibji, isn't that very strange?'

'It is.'

'But why, Sahibji? Why do such a foolish thing?' Om Prakash continues, oblivious to Vikram's growing discomfort.

'How does it matter to us?'

'Sorry, Sahibji.'

Vikram relents. 'It's all right,' he says, and puts a hand on Om Prakash's shoulder. 'It is believed that in one of their very early matches – some time around 1880, I think – Australia thrashed England. The English public was so upset by the defeat that they said it was the death of English cricket, that it would be cremated, and the ashes would be taken to Australia.'

Om Prakash shrugs. 'Thank you, Sahibji,' he says.

Eight and a half hours from when they left the cremation ground, Neera, Ketaki, Vikram, and Om Prakash approach their destination. To avoid the pandits and the protracted pujas, the homeless and the general mayhem that are Haridwar, they locate a deserted ghat on the outskirts of the city. With the ashes and the bones, the four stand quietly, heads bent, before a restive Ganga. Neera steps away. She finds a spot under the shade of a tree.

'I will take a dip, then we will do the immersion,' Om Prakash says. In a matter of seconds, he strips down to his underclothes, scrambles into the river, closes his nose, takes three full dips, and runs out again. He pulls out a large rag from the trunk of the car, dries himself, and dresses. 'Now let us say the Gayatri Mantra and immerse the flowers.'

The three of them look to Neera, who shakes her head and waves them away. Ketaki, Vikram, and Om Prakash roll up their trousers and wade into the river. Knee-deep in water, they recite the mantra and release the bones and ashes into the Ganga. Ketaki turns around: Her aunt is still sitting under the tree. Distant yet intensely forlorn, Neera looks back at her.

14

It is either hot or cold in Delhi; spring and autumn do not exist as seasons, but as days of pleasant weather that can be counted on one's fingers. It was on one such day at the end of March, on the cusp between winter and summer, when Ketaki and Siddharth broke up. Deepak was still alive then.

Siddharth had come over to pick up some of the paintings they had selected to have them framed. He walked into her flat, made himself some coffee, and sat down in the studio. As he flipped through the paintings, deciding which ones to get framed first, she grabbed his coffee mug and smashed it to the floor. He jumped up from the stool and looked at her. She looked back at him and said that she could not do this. Why didn't you tell me straight that you don't want to do the show? he said. No, not the show, she said. I mean this, us.

He did not ask why. Instead, he chewed at his bottom lip for a while, nodded his head, then said, I guess you're just not ready for a serious relationship. And with that quick-fix deduction, he was able to file away the episode for current relief and future use, then hug her and turn towards the door. Could I get you another mug of coffee? she asked as he was walking out. No, thank you, he replied, and left to become one more memory.

It was that simple. Naturally, her initial relief turned, curdling into a glob that sat in her gut and made her bilious. But it passed quite quickly. Within a few days she was more or less functional again. Now, however, her uncle is gone, her aunt teeters between catatonic and hyperactive states, and her father is here and in no rush to leave.

She was planning to work for a bit before going back to her aunt's for dinner, but the electricity has gone. It goes off every night during the summer months, when temperatures touch forty-five Celsius and humidity hangs at around ninety per cent. They call it load-shedding. If she is lucky, it will only be gone an hour.

She fetches a couple of ice trays from the freezer, tosses them into a bucketful of water, and by candlelight she bathes. Once cooled, she steps out of the bath and slips on an old sundress over her wet body. She walks out into the passage and fumbles with the inverter, hoping that a little kicking, some shaking, some switching on and off will get the thing to work. It will not. With no fan and no light, her only option is to go outside.

The terrace is not much cooler, the din and diesel fumes of neighbouring generators aggravate, but at least the air moves and there is some visibility in the early evening gloaming. Resting against the terrace railing smoking a cigarette, she views the activity on the street. Everyone without power back-up is out in their gardens, or on verandahs, patios, rooftops. On the terrace in front of her, shirtless Mr Chatterji is no longer so. He is dressed in a freshly laundered inhibition. Next to him sits his wife, a large steel colander on her lap, deveining prawns. Mrs Chatterji looks at Ketaki, then at her husband, then at Ketaki again. Ketaki smiles; Mrs Chatterji returns to her prawns.

The electricity eventually returns at seven thirty, a good hour and a half after it went, and Ketaki is confronted with the task of getting back to work, something she has not done in a while. It has been a fortnight since her uncle died, and she has still not stepped into the studio. There has just been something or other going on at her aunt's. There have been the visitors coming to condole, a constant flow of them, which has only slowed now. Then there is her father, who is staying at Neera's and with whom Ketaki feels compelled to spend time. And finally, of course, there is Neera: Neera who will sit all day in a still and silent stupor, then suddenly rise and rush to the garage to rummage all night through her husband's things; Neera who will not eat and cannot sleep.

Ketaki unbolts the door to the studio, walks in, and switches on the lights, the air conditioner, and her computer. As the Mac starts up, she swivels around on her chair to face the entire breadth of the room. In the middle of the studio that Deepak built sits the drawing board that Krishan made upon which are stacked the paintings that Siddharth selected. Lars is out of this picture, she thinks. Ketaki turns back to the monitor and stares at it as her cluttered desktop loads up. Slumped over the table with her hand on the mouse, she moseys about the blank screen of a browser window with the cursor, watching it switch from arrow to hand to arrow again and again and again. She closes her eyes, pushes the mouse away, and slowly spins around on her chair. Giddy after several rotations, she stops. Her eyes open. She brings the cursor to the iPhoto icon on her desktop, then quickly moves it away. Fuck this, she thinks, and gets up.

•

Neera and Vikram are in the study watching an IPL cricket match when Ketaki comes in. The Deccan Chargers are playing Kings XI Punjab.

'No prizes for guessing which team will win,' Vikram says, rising from his chair to give his daughter a hug. 'I think the Chargers have barely won a game.'

Neera's eyes briefly meet Ketaki's, then return to the cricket match.

Ketaki sits down on the sofa by her aunt. 'Why do you have a sheet over you?' she says. 'Are you feeling cold?'

'Laxman… useless captain,' Neera says, her voice feeble. 'And paid one and a half crores.'

'Your masi is running a fever, I think,' Vikram says. 'And she's refusing to check her temperature.'

'Gilchrist out for six,' she whispers, her eyes still locked on the TV.

'Neera, do you remember that test match we went to in '72?' Vikram says.

Neera turns her head and looks at him absently.

'India versus England?'

'Chandrasekhar,' she says, barely audible.

'Pardon?' Vikram says.

'Chandrasekhar,' she repeats, only marginally louder.

Vikram guffaws. 'Yes, exactly. Chandrasekhar, the legendary leg-spinner,' he says. 'Ketu, you should have seen your Neera Masi there. Neera, are you going to tell her?'

Neera looks at Ketaki with a little girl's eyes.

'Chandrasekhar had got three wickets in just ten balls,' Vikram says.

'Eight,' Neera mumbles.

'Eight balls, correct, and – '

'And Wood and Fletcher and Lewis. Wood and Fletcher and Lewis out in eight balls.'

'And?' Vikram says, prompting her.

'Chandrasekhar.'

'Yes, and tell Ketu what happened next.'

'Chandrasekhar crushed England's batting.'

'And, Ketu, your masi got so excited that she leapt up from her seat, jumped up and down wildly, and then suddenly bang! She fell and broke her ankle.'

Neera looks away from the TV and towards the window. 'Deep carried me to the car,' she says, as if in a trance, as if by mere sight the neem tree outside holds her in its sway.

'Yes, but not before getting you Chandrasekhar's autograph!' Vikram says, laughing. 'Your masi refused to leave without the autograph – even though she was in complete agony with her ankle!'

'Deep carried me to the car,' she says again.

'Deepak did – and it must have been at least half a kilometre.'

'Yes,' Neera says. 'He picked me up and carried me to the car.' She pulls the sheet up to her chin.

'Your masi was a total cricket buff, Ketu.' Vikram says. 'Deepak would try and take her to all the test matches.'

'Bombay. Kanpur. Madras,' Neera recites.

'Deepak took her everywhere,' Vikram says. 'I don't know how many international tests they saw.'

'Bangalore. Calcutta…'

'Calcutta! I remember when we all went to Calcutta for the West Indies series,' Vikram says.

'December,' Neera says. 'December 1974.'

'It was the four of us again,' Vikram says. 'The two crazy Mehra sisters and their husbands.'

'India won,' Neera says.

'That was a wonderful trip,' Vikram says. 'Calcutta had so much charm then.'

'West Indies batted badly,' Neera says.

'They were overconfident,' Vikram says. 'I think it was Lloyd who made a fatal mistake.'

'Chandrasekhar,' Neera says.

Vikram tilts his head back. 'Was it Chandrasekhar?' he says. 'Yes, of course it was. What a ball that was…'

'Bowled Lloyd off his pads,' Neera says.

'Ketu, you see how cricket-crazy your masi was?'

'We won a prize for dancing,' Neera says. 'Deep and I.'

Vikram sits up and smacks his thigh. 'You did, I remember! At the New Year's Eve bash. You should have seen your aunt and uncle, Ketu – they set the dance floor on fire!'

Neera turns, her abstracted eyes settle on Ketaki. 'Best dance couple award,' she says. 'Dinner for two at Park Hotel.'

'Maybe you should take up dancing again,' Ketaki says.

The left side of Neera's mouth curls into what could be a half-smile.

'I think that's a great idea,' Vikram says. 'Maybe aunt and niece should sign up for dance classes together.'

'And how come you don't watch cricket anymore?' Ketaki says.

'I do,' her aunt says. 'When I have the time.'

'But you never go for any matches,' Ketaki says.

'Too much of a bother. Parking, security, junglee crowds.'

'Come on, Masi. What about if we go to see an IPL match?'

'I don't like T20. It's not real cricket. It's just a show – Bollywood cricket.'

'Masi...'

'It's getting a little cold in the room,' Neera says.

'Should I get the thermometer?' Ketaki says.

'I'm fine,' her aunt says.

'Should I switch the AC off?' Vikram says.

'Yes,' Neera says. 'Thank you.'

'Not a problem,' Vikram says, getting up.

'But I have plans,' Neera says.

'Pardon?' Vikram says, sitting down again.

'Plans?' Ketaki says, turning to her aunt.

Neera tries to straighten up. 'Yes, plans,' she says. 'A cottage on my plot in Pangot.' She looks at Ketaki, then at Vikram.

'That sounds like a very good idea,' Vikram says.

'Yes. My dream cottage in the hills,' Neera says. She turns again to Ketaki.

Ketaki picks up the TV remote and increases the volume.

'I have an architect. Sheila, Sheila Seth's son.'

'He doesn't do residential projects,' Ketaki says.

'He said he'll make an exception. He's very excited about it.'

'This is very exciting,' Vikram says.

'Two cottages,' Neera says. 'One for myself, one for a little hotel.'

'That's a great idea,' Vikram says.

'I'm going to build two cottages – the property is large enough for two. One for myself, a small cottage for myself, a kind of annexe – two bedrooms with two attached bathrooms, a kitchen, a drawing-cum-dining room – and then a larger one with four or five bedrooms that I could run as a hotel.'

'That's a great idea,' Vikram says again, beaming. 'What do you think, Ketu?'

'Clearly it's all planned out,' Ketaki says, rolling her eyes.

'I don't know, that's what I'm thinking. I've always wanted to do it,' her aunt says. 'No, but yes... yes, I'm going to do something like that. I'm going to do something like that finally.'

The woman is crazy, Ketaki thinks, as she tosses about bare-bodied in a hot bed. She is out of her fucking mind. Moving to the hills – a hotel! What the hell is she thinking? She will never manage. How can she? Not at her age. Not by herself. First she would have to construct it, then set it up, get permissions, arrange electricity and water connections, hire people, run the place. There is no way, there is no fucking way she could manage.

Grief has exhausted Neera of good sense, Ketaki resolves. Grief is known to turn the most reasonable of human beings into crazies. But once her aunt is back to normal all those dumb-ass plans will be forgotten. She will be back to her usual self, her usual life of magazines and Scrabble and coffee mornings and evening concerts.

Ketaki gets up and opens the window to let in the marginally cooler air from outside, but all that comes through are the shrill, crackly wails of an all-night prayer meeting jettisoned from some ancient loudspeaker. She shuts the window, turns on the air conditioner, and calls Krishan.

Krishan comes over only on the condition that she god promises and mother swears that she is no longer attached to some other man. As soon as she makes her avowals of singlehood, his jeans are off.

'So, what happened?' he says, as soon as he pulls out of her.

'What happened?' she says. 'Nothing happened. It was great. I haven't come like that in a long time.'

'No, man, I mean with that boy you were meeting – Aditya?'

'Siddharth.'

'Yes, yes, Siddharth.'

She sits up and lights a cigarette.

'Still smoking?'

'Yes.'

'So, what happened?'

'We broke up about a month ago.'

'But what happened?'

'Nothing, nothing really. He was a nice guy. It just didn't work out.'

'What does it mean, It just didn't work out?' Krishan says. 'All the time in those TV programmes on Star World people say, It just didn't work out. I don't understand it.'

'What's there not to understand?' she says. 'It is what it is. The relationship didn't work out.'

'I don't believe that stuff, yaar. I think people say that when there is no proper reason. And I think that most of the time people have no proper reasons – no proper problems.'

She rolls onto him. 'Tell me more, guruji,' she says.

'This is not a joke,' he says, pushing her off him. 'I am being very serious.'

'Okay,' she says, lying on her back.

He turns onto his side and looks at her. 'See, the problem is not the boy or the girl. The problem is choice. In these modern days there is too much choice. When we have so many choices we always think there is someone better, prettier, sweeter. It is the same with jobs, man. I see my friends. They work in call centres for some time, then they think they can do something better, then they work in a hotel or an airline company or in computers, then again they think it is not so good and again move. They are never happy. Too much choice.'

'So you're saying that I'm spoilt for choice?' She laughs.

'You think all this is funny?' he says, shifting onto his back. 'Be serious, man. This is not a laughing matter.'

'I'm sorry, I wasn't laughing at you.'

'Okay,' he says, on his side again, facing her. 'And see, the problem is not just too much choice. The problem is also that us youngsters don't know how to make choices. Nowadays the fashion is love marriage but I still think arranged marriage is the best way. My friends laugh at me, they call me Papaji. But I don't care. See, we Indians always try to be like the Westerners, but we – especially us youngsters – we forget that our parents have much knowledge and experience. They know what is good for us. And nowadays they are less strict. No more of that thing when the girl used to come in the veil and the father of the boy forced him to marry her. Nowadays parents see the best combo for their child and then give him the full right to say yes or no. And not just boys, even girls. Parents don't force the children, they only guide. We need to take guidance to make our choice – for marriage, for job, everything. Without guidance from our elders we make too many mistakes.'

'You're probably right,' she says.

Krishan rolls onto his back. 'See, after my BA I thought I would do training to become a flight steward. I thought the salary was good and I could travel and get free air tickets for my family. But Daddyji was very against it. He said it was just like being a bearer, a bearer in the air. And he said there is a readymade family business and I will be a stupid fool to just leave that and be a silly bearer in a suit. In the beginning I was fighting with him. No! I will do what I want to do! You can't force me! But then thank god in the end I listened. Now, today, I am in my daddy's business. Slowly, slowly I am trying to make it bigger, I am trying to do more so my daddy can also take more holidays and enjoy a little. Sometimes it is boring, sometimes Daddyji and I fight, but see, it is the same for all my friends who keep changing jobs. But my life is not so problematic as their lives. They are always looking for better choices, but me? Me, I have quite a simple, easy life. I think I am happier.' He looks at her and smiles. 'Too much lecturing, no?' he says.

'No,' she says. 'Not at all.'

'Then can I say one last thing?'

'Sure,' she says, lighting up again.

'See, this thing that you and I do, this is different to marriage. This is play. From time to time we meet and so that is why it is great fun. We don't have to buy vegetables and get rations and look after parents and in-laws and family. But marriage cannot be like this. People say that there has to be passion and chemistry. That is only bonus. Marriage has to be understanding and sacrifice.' He sits up.

'That's probably right.'

'Are you going to push me out of your flat now?'

'No,' she says, 'not yet.'

He lies down again and rolls towards her. 'One more time then?'

15

At around eleven the next morning Vikram shows up at her flat. It is too early in the day for civility; much too early for parental ministrations, parental counsel or care. But Vikram is happy to amuse himself with the newspaper while she washes off the morning grumps in the bath.

Guidance is what Krishan called it. Take guidance from your elders, he said. Yes, she thinks, as she soaps herself, take guidance from your elders and all will be well, every choice made will be the right one. But choice? How much of where she is, of what she is, is actually a product of choice? Mostly it is a by-product of chance – the chance of being born to that man sitting out in the living room. But screw facticity – screw Sartre and Heidegger. She needs to get out of the bath, dry off, and engage with that man.

'Neera's not doing very well,' Vikram says to her as she comes into the living room armed with a mug of coffee. 'She's running a high fever, she can't get out of bed.'

'She seemed all right last evening,' Ketaki says. 'She was quite chirpy talking about cricket and dancing – and her Pangot plans.'

'I think she knows how to pretend,' Vikram says. 'Gopal Singh slept outside her room. He said the lights were on all night. I don't think she slept a wink.'

Ketaki takes a sip of her coffee.

'Do you think you could stay over tonight? I'm a little worried about her.'

'I don't know,' she says. 'Let's see.'

'Only if it suits you. If you've got plans for the evening, don't worry about it.'

'I don't have plans.'

'Good,' Vikram says. 'In fact, Prakash Bhapa and Usha are coming over for dinner.'

She sets her mug down on the floor. 'Do you think Masi's actually serious about the cottage in Pangot?'

'I think so.'

'But why? Why now?'

'She's always wanted to move to the hills – that's why she bought the property with the money Nanima left her. But I think Deepak was never keen. He loved the mountains, but he never actually wanted to live there.'

'But at this age?' Ketaki says.

'Why not? We're not that old, darling.'

'I know, but how would she manage?'

'She'll manage just fine,' Vikram says. 'And I'd be happy to help her in any way. I think it would be very good for her.'

'All by herself in the hills – I don't know.'

'Maybe you could spend time with her there.'

'Me?' Ketaki says. 'No way. And anyhow, she hasn't even asked me.'

'You know you don't have to be asked. It's your Neera Masi we're talking about.'

'I don't know,' she says.

'Are you upset by her decision?'

'Upset? Please. I just think it's foolish. And it's too soon – Deepak Uncle has been gone barely two weeks. I don't think she's in any condition to make any major plans right now.'

Vikram leans forward in his chair. 'What about you?' he says. 'Do you have any plans?'

'Not really,' Ketaki says.

'How about New York?'

'What?'

'Coming back to New York. You know your job with Max is always there – he still keeps asking about you – and – '

'Papa, please.'

'I'm sorry,' Vikram says. 'I don't give up, do I?'

'That's okay.'

'Or at least come to visit. Spend a little time and then decide whether you could live there again.'

'I don't know, Papa,' she says. 'I really don't know.'

'Just think about it. Think about it without pressure.'

'Okay.' She moves to the floor and lies down flat on her back on the carpet.

'You must miss Deepak a lot,' her father says.

Lifting her head up, she looks at him. 'What do you mean?' she says.

'He was like a father to you,' Vikram says.

She sets her head down on the carpet again and closes her eyes. He. Was. Like. A. Father. To. You. Seven words. Just seven words. But the semantic possibilities, the ambiguities are endless. Better, then, to remain quiet.

'Ketu?'

'Yes?'

'Are you all right?'

'Yes,' she says, sitting up. 'I'm sorry, but I need to go. I have lunch plans with Adil.'

•

'They were voted Most Significant Pest/Problem in Australia,' Ketaki says, as she and Adil watch a local of mynas loiter outside in the restaurant's patio.

'They have polls like that in Australia?' Adil says.

She laughs. 'They claim that Indian mynas threaten native species, damage crops, cause noise pollution, blah blah blah. They have hate groups for the poor birds. Indian mynas are rats in the sky! The plague! I found a website – mynamagnet or something – where they have nasty contraptions to kill them – traps, gassing bags, gassing hoses that can be attached to your car's exhaust.'

'So this is for Indian mynas, right?'

'Yes,' she says, finishing up her goat cheese soufflé.

'Racists,' he says, smiling. 'Dessert?'

'No, thank you, but you go ahead.'

'I'm done.'

'So, they were brought from India in very small numbers in the late eighteen hundreds – to control insects in agricultural areas,' she says. 'But they were so amazingly adaptable that they spread all over the country.'

'We're still talking about birds, right?'

Ketaki gives him a little kick under the table. 'Speaking of Indian migratory habits,' she says, 'my dad was over at my place this morning. He was trying to get me to come to New York.'

'Are you planning to go?'

'I don't know. I'll see how things go. But then he asked me if I miss Deepak Uncle,' she says. 'It was strange.'

'Strange?' Adil says, folding his napkin.

'Just an odd thing to ask me.'

'It's a perfectly natural question.'

'No. It's like he suspects something.'

'Suspects what?' Adil says.

'Maybe he also thinks I had something going on with Deepak.'

'Maybe you're getting a little carried away.'

'Well, my aunt suspects it,' Ketaki says. 'She said that Deepak was trying to mould me into my mother.'

Adil looks at her questioningly.

'She was basically saying that once my mother died, he needed to replace her. He tried to make me into her. He tried to get me to do the things she did – the birding, the art, the tennis, and god knows what else.'

'Did she actually say that?'

'She said that he tried to make me Uma, but whether he succeeded or not, she did not know.' Ketaki pulls a drinking straw out of its holder and taps it against the table. 'It's like she was saying that he was trying to make me into his lover.'

'You – '

'I wasn't his lover,' she says. 'Not ever. For fuck's sake, he's my uncle.'

Adil takes the straw from her hand and puts it down on his side plate.

'Sometimes I hate him, you know. I also feel stupid – stupid for allowing myself to be made into my mother.'

'But each of us grows in the likeness of someone else, isn't it?' Adil says. 'We're all created in the image of another, and usually it's a parent. Role models. Only sometimes we don't choose them – they're chosen for us.'

She pulls out another straw. 'What a role model I have,' she says.

'But honestly,' Adil says, 'I don't think your dad suspects that there was something on between you and your uncle. If anything, he probably just feels he wants to be a better father, like he feels your uncle was with you.'

217

'I don't know. Anyway, screw it. She's dead, he's dead. It's over. Okay, I think I need coffee. Would you like one too?'

Adil waves out to a waiter and places their order.

'I feel like I need to do something,' she says. 'I mean, what am I doing? What the fuck am I doing?' She rubs her face with her hands.

He looks at her, reaches for her hands, holds them.

'Even my aunt has plans. She's all set to move to the hills.'

'Really?'

'Yes,' Ketaki says. 'She wants to start up a small hotel in Pangot.'

'Pangot?'

'Up in the hills in Uttaranchal. Anyway, I don't even know if that'll actually happen. Right now she's in a state. I don't think she's capable of making rational decisions.'

The coffee arrives.

'But I just don't know what I'm doing,' Ketaki says, dumping three teaspoonfuls of sugar into her espresso. 'I can't work, I can't think, I can't do anything.'

Head tipped to his left, Adil looks at her.

'What?' she says.

'Nothing. I was just thinking... I was just thinking about how when my father died, my mother just sort of got on with things,' Adil says. 'Of course it took her a while, but she actively tried to get her life back together. She made plans with her sisters, travelled all over, played Bridge every afternoon.' He gazes into his coffee cup. 'Meanwhile, I just floundered. Floundered for months. I missed him, but I hated myself for missing him. I tried to forget him, but I hated myself for that too. I couldn't work, I didn't want to do anything, I couldn't see anyone. But in the end it came to the same thing. My mother and I had completely different ways of handling the situation, but finally it came to the same thing. We both changed in order to adjust to my father's absence – it's just that with her it was something more or less consciously done, whereas for myself the change happened in the wallowing, the change happened insidiously.'

'What about your brother?' she says.

'What about him?'

'How did he feel?'

'I don't know.'

'You don't know?'

Adil looks up from his cup and his eyes settle at some point between her nose and chin. 'He didn't come for the funeral. He said that the school's final exams were going on and he couldn't come.'

'Okay.'

'And when he came six months later it was as if nothing had happened. Not a word was said about my father or his dying.'

'That must have been strange,' she says.

'But anyway,' Adil says, picking up his coffee cup, 'as I was saying, I don't think you should be made to feel pressure in trying to cope, in trying to change. You can't force it. You can't rush it. For some people it takes a while, but the transformation eventually happens, the adjustments take place, albeit a little slowly.'

'True.'

'Which is not to say that a little self-reflection is harmful,' he says, smiling.

She smiles back. 'My very own personal life coach,' she says, and kisses him on the edge of his mouth.

•

A face that showed beauty just a day ago, a face that must have been called gorgeous in its springtide, now rests in a pillow, pallid, covered by the grey film of a high fever.

'Masi?'

The eyes open haltingly, look up at Ketaki standing over the bed, gradually begin to focus.

'It's nine fifteen, Masi. You need to have your dinner.'

Neera closes her eyes again.

'Gopal Singh is bringing you some rice and dal.'

She shakes her head.

'Come on, I'll help you up.' Ketaki sits down by the edge of the bed and tries to pull her aunt up by the shoulders.

'No,' Neera says, her body going rigid.

Ketaki sets her aunt down again.

'Prakash Mama and Usha Mami have been here since seven thirty and we should probably have dinner served soon.'

'Yes,' Neera wheezes. 'It will get late for the servants.'

'But you need to eat first,' Ketaki says. 'Once you're finished I'll have dinner put on the table for them.'

'I can't.'

'You've got to eat. You can't take your medicines on an empty stomach.'

'I ate lunch.'

'Papa said you had half a chapati.'

'I'll come to the table.'

'You need to rest.'

'I can't eat in bed.'

'Are you sure? I don't think you should be moving around.'

Neera nods.

'Okay, I'll help you up.' Ketaki extends a hand.

'No, I'll do it,' her aunt says.

Ketaki withdraws.

Turning to her side, Neera drops her legs off the bed and slowly pushes herself up to a sitting position. She attempts a few deep breaths, then irons down her caftan with her hands. 'Could I have my hairbrush please?' she says.

Ketaki fetches the brush from the dressing table.

'Thank you,' Neera says. 'You go ahead, I'll join you at the table.'

Hair groomed, lipstick applied, her pink caftan smoothed down, Neera enters the dining room dressed in her pretences. She comes around to greet Prakash and Usha, before Vikram pulls her chair out and she assumes her seat at the head of the table.

'Look at you, Neera dear,' Usha says. 'Looking so weak.'

'I'm fine,' Neera says.

'No, you must be careful,' Usha says. 'This viral is really going around. Just last week your brother had it. Terrible. High fever – '

'Break-bone fever,' Prakash says.

'Just terrible,' Usha continues. 'His temperature stayed above one hundred and one for five days continuously.'

'That's awful,' Vikram says.

'I gave him a lot of cooling foods – dahi, buttermilk, light fruits – only then he got better. No, Daddy?'

'Yes,' Prakash says. 'Nourishment is key. Keta, you need to be more strict with your masi. You have to make her eat.'

'I'm eating, I'm eating,' Neera says, dawdling with her fork.

'She's trying, Prakash Bhapa,' Vikram says, 'and Ketu and I will do the best we can to get her well.'

After dinner, a feast for all but one, the party proceeds to the study. Neera, who insists on staying up a while, is made to lie on the sofa; the others assemble around her. A singing session ensues, Prakash on lead vocals, his wife on backup.

It is Rafi–Naushad night, Prakash declares at the start, and the family is treated to a string of film songs composed by the greatest music director Naushad Ali and sung by legend of all legends Mohammed Rafi. Before every song he is about to perform, Prakash launches forth on its provenance: the lyricist, the film for which it was composed, the year the film was released, the cast, the 'picturization' of the song.

Prakash is at the coda of 'Suhaani raat dhal chuki', what he had introduced as an immortal masterpiece, when Neera interrupts. 'Prakash Bhapa,' she says, heaving herself into a seated posture, '"Na tum humein jaano".'

Usha shifts in her chair, Vikram looks down at his shoes.

'"Na tum humein jaano"?' Prakash says.

'Yes,' Neera says. 'The song you used to sing for Deepak and me.'

He looks at Usha, who tries to come to the rescue: 'But dear, that's a Hemant Kumar song,' she says. 'We're doing Rafi–Naushad tonight.'

'I know,' Neera says. 'But could you?'

'Are you sure?' Prakash says.

'I promise not to cry, if that's what you're worried about,' Neera says.

Prakash smiles weakly, clears his throat and begins, humming the first few bars of the song, as in the original rendition. Then he stops. He stops and looks around.

'What happened?' Neera says. 'It's beautiful. Please continue.'

With a deep breath he starts again, humming the introduction, faltering into its refrain, and finally, hesitatingly, embarking on the first verse. His eyes resting on Neera, he sings of the quiet night, the quiet lips, the silence that tells the story.

Neera sways slowly to the tune with her eyes closed, mouthing the words with Prakash. Even after the song is over she continues to sway as if held in a narcotic rapture until Ketaki puts a hand on her arm. Neera opens her eyes.

'You've probably been up too long,' Vikram says to her. 'Maybe you need to turn in now.'

'Yes,' she says, lifting herself of the sofa. 'I'm tired.' She says her goodbyes and allows Ketaki to escort her to the bedroom.

The song stays with Neera as she prepares for bed. From outside the bathroom door Ketaki can hear her aunt's humming even over the loud hiss of her pee. The delirium persists in bed as she continues to hum with the thermometer in her mouth.

'Masi, stop,' Ketaki says. 'We won't get a correct reading.'

Neera obliges, staring at her niece, until the thermometer is taken out.

'It's a hundred and two, Masi,' Ketaki says, viewing the thin silver line of mercury.

'Oopsy,' Neera says.

Ketaki scowls at her aunt's choice of expression. 'Two Crocins then,' she says.

'Yes.'

Once she has settled her aunt into bed, Ketaki goes to the cupboard, pulls out one of Neera's old kurtas, changes, and gets into bed.

'What are you doing?' Neera says.

'I'm staying over,' Ketaki says, lying on her back.

'Why?'

'You tell me.'

'It's not needed,' Neera says.

'Go to sleep.'

'I'm not sleepy.'

'I'm putting the light off,' Ketaki says.

'Not yet.'

'Do you need something?'

'No.'

'Then?'

Neera pulls out a handkerchief from under her pillow and wipes her mouth. 'Then nothing,' she says.

Ketaki turns onto her side. 'Are you okay?' she says.

'I'm fine.'

Lying face to face, each woman with her legs curled, her head resting in the palm of her hand, they look at each other.

'You need to sleep,' Ketaki says after two or three quiet minutes, and without waiting for an answer, she kisses her aunt on the cheek and switches off the light.

'Keta?'

Ketaki moves closer to her aunt until Neera's dry, hot breath is upon her face, but she does not respond.

'Keta?' Neera says again.

'What Masi?'

Neera fumbles for Ketaki's hand in the dark and holds it to her chest.

Ketaki switches the bedside lamp on again. 'Are you okay?' she says.

Squinting in the light, Neera nods.

'Why can't you sleep?'

'Do you miss your uncle?'

Ketaki pulls her hand away and rolls onto her back.

'Do you miss your uncle?'

'Why are you asking me this?'

'This has been difficult for you,' Neera says. 'I've been difficult.'

Ketaki sits up. 'I don't know if I miss him,' she says.

'He loved you.'

'It doesn't matter.'

'He did.'

Ketaki looks down at her aunt.

'But you're right. We should sleep,' Neera says.

'Do you miss him?' Ketaki says.

'You know, this hanky,' Neera says, unclenching her fist to reveal her handkerchief, 'Deepak Uncle bought it for me when he went to Brussels. Belgian Lace.' She wipes her mouth with it again. 'It's pretty, isn't it?'

Ketaki lies down again and turns towards her aunt.

'I miss him,' Neera says. 'Isn't that odd?'

'Should I put the light off?'

'Yes.'

Ketaki turns off the light for a second time.

'Good night,' Neera says, and once more takes Ketaki's hand and holds it close to her chest.

16

Vikram has been dropped off at the airport, and Ketaki and Om Prakash are driving back to Panchsheel. The air conditioner has been cranked up in the car, although it does little to keep out the mid-afternoon burn. But even in June, the cruellest month of the year, when the searing dust winds from the west blow, even so, Delhi is in flower, refulgent with the magentas and yellows and oranges of bougainvillea, laburnum, and gulmohar that burgeon in this deathly blaze.

Her father has finally left, now that his brother-in-law's papers have been put in order, his sister-in-law is convalescing, and his daughter – well, he tried, he certainly tried, but his daughter is a basket case and nothing can really be done about her. So, jobs done, he has taken flight, gone, gone to get on with his life.

And why not? Why be like Neera who built herself a little hell in which she locked herself up? But at least she was real about it; she looked at the problem squarely – though that was all she did. Eyes so firmly fixed on the problem, she never saw what was around her, she never saw ahead. Vikram, meanwhile, fled, made a little make-believe life for himself. So then which is better? Her nether world or his wonderland?

Vikram was young, though; he was just forty-one when

Uma died and not even fifty when he met Megan. Maybe Deepak should have died years ago too. Not when Neera is sixty. Not when she has had to endure him for so long. Now it is too late; the damage is done. Now all that Neera can do is cook up harebrained fantasies – plans, she called them! – of a little mountain cottage in Pangot and a quaint little hotel. But for her to move on at this age and after what she has been through? And for her to find another man? Even if she did, to what purpose? Love? Sex? Maybe she will find herself a hot little Gurkha in Pangot.

'What's happened, Baby?' Om Prakash says, looking at Ketaki through the rear-view mirror. 'You seem to be in deep thought.'

'Nothing,' she says. 'I'm fine.'

It was two and a half years ago, in January 2006, that Ketaki returned to India after nine years in New York. It was not as if she had planned a final comeback – she was merely on her annual visit to Delhi to see her aunt and uncle. However, instead of going back to New York a month later as she had done in years past, this time around she stayed. One month became three, three became six, until one fine morning she woke up and realized that this was it, this was home, this was where she wanted to be. Deepak found her a flat five houses down the street, just around this time in June two years ago, settled her in, helped her find work, and that was that.

At the time, Vikram was deeply saddened by her decision. He could not understand why his daughter would want to leave New York – she had a great job with a top design house, a nice circle of friends, a lovely apartment, and she had him, her father. Most of what he said was true, but what he failed to see was that in all that she had, one thing was missing: Deepak.

Of course, within a few months Vikram did come around. He has tried on occasion to ask her to rethink her decision, but as such he does not put any pressure on her. As for Ketaki, she finds it hard to tell whether her decision to move to India was a correct one or not. But does it matter? One is prone to think that every decision you make will have far-reaching consequences, but is that really the case? How different would her life have been if she remained in New York?

But now Deepak is dead. The reason for her decision is dead. Does that mean she should just go back to New York? Would Lars be waiting for her? Would he thrust aside the woman he is with and gather Ketaki into his arms?

'Baby, I've known you from the day you were born,' Om Prakash says, as they wait at a traffic light near the Malai Mandir, 'I've carried you in my arms. I know something is troubling you.'

Ketaki smiles. 'No, nothing. I'm just feeling sleepy.'

'Say what you want,' he says, 'but you can't hide anything from me.'

On their way to the airport Vikram asked her about the show. It pissed her off. In the whole month that he had been here he had not bothered to ask her about it. He had not even asked to see his wife's paintings. But Ketaki did not react to his question. She shrugged it off and turned to the window. I really think it's a wonderful idea, he persisted, and you don't need Siddharth to do it – I'll help you. I truly mean it, Ketu, he said, it's a wonderful idea. Not only is it a way for you to showcase your work, it might also help you to forgive Mummy.

Forgive Mummy? she thinks. Forgiveness makes her nervous. It demands some kind of moral authority on the part of the forgiver that makes her uncomfortable. But truth be told, the impulse to forgive is strong. Is that how it is with families? To forgive and so to forget? That said, what is there to forgive? Uma needs to be blamed for something first, so that Ketaki may forgive her. What should Ketaki blame her mother for?

That she smokes too much, chews her nails, and slacks off work – should she blame her mother for that? She does not seem to stick it out with a man for too long. Should she blame her mother for that? She has trouble engaging with her father, trouble engaging with her aunt. Should she blame her mother for that? She lost Deepak, the person she loved most. Can she blame her mother for that?

Ketaki rolls down her window and lights up a cigarette.

Om Prakash scowls at her through the rear-view mirror. 'Look at yourself,' he says. 'You don't listen to anyone. Smoking cigarettes like a man. Madam doesn't smoke. Mataji never smoked, but look at you.'

'Mummy smoked.'

'Your mummy,' he says, shaking his head, 'your dear mummy. But so what? If your mummy jumped in a well would you also jump in a well?'

Maybe I would, she thinks. I have been groomed into being her, so maybe I would.

Ketaki sticks her head out of the window, heedless of the hot loo outside. Mummy, she thinks. Dear, dear mummy.

She opens the door before he rings the bell. Without a word, she grabs his hand and drags him into the studio. Still holding onto him she rolls a chair from the desk to the drawing board. 'Sit,' she says.

'Thank you,' he says, taking a seat. 'What about you?'

'I'm okay,' she says. 'Drink?'

'I'm good.'

Adil's eyes follow her around as she pulls out a file, puts it back in, walks up to the window, then returns to his side.

'A very nice workspace you have here,' he says.

'Thank you. My uncle had it built.'

'Yes, I remember you mentioning that.'

'He had it especially constructed for me,' she says, hovering about Adil. 'You like it?'

'Very much,' he says. 'Why don't you sit down?'

She perches herself on the high stool next to him.

'How are you doing?' he says.

'Good. Good, thanks,' she says, reaching for her sketchpad.

'Everything all right?'

She takes a charcoal stick and begins to draw.

'How's your aunt?'

'Okay.'

'Your father?'

'My dad's left,' she says, looking up at him. 'Things are getting back to normal. Masi's feeling better, Deepak Uncle's paperwork has been put in order. Everything's in place.' She returns to her sketchpad.

'How are you feeling?' Adil says.

'I'm okay. I'm doing okay.'

'What are you sketching there?'

She lifts up the pad and shows him the drawing.

'Who's that?' he says.

'I don't know.' She tears the sheet off and crumples it up. 'Vita brevis, ars brevis,' she says with a smirk.

'All right.'

'My dad,' she says, 'my dad thinks I should still do the show.'

'What do you think?' Adil says.

'I can't do it,' Ketaki says.

'Why?'

'I can't,' she says, kicking the drawing board with her foot. 'Isn't that why Siddharth and I broke up?'

'Is it?'

'Siddharth said it's a way to celebrate her – to bring her back to life. But Mummy's already here,' Ketaki says, pointing to her head. 'Here,' she says again, now hitting her head over and over again with her sketchpad. 'She's here and everywhere, and...'

Adil takes the pad from her and puts it down on the floor.

'She's supposed to be dead – and I want her to remain dead,' Ketaki says, suddenly vaulting off the stool. It tumbles over with a loud clunk. 'I'm sorry,' she says, stepping away.

'It's okay,' Adil says, lifting the stool up.

'But Papa thinks I should do the show as... I don't know... some sort of act of forgiveness or something.'

'Forgiveness?'

'Yes,' she says, walking around the drawing board. 'But you know what? When it comes down to it, when I really think about it, there's almost nothing about Mummy that I really find blameworthy. So she slept with Deepak Uncle, so she had some long, passionate affair with him. But can I blame her? Can I blame him? I don't know. If I were in some lousy marriage, would I do the same? I mean this whole notion of forgiveness... it's bullshit.' Her fist comes crashing down on the stool. 'I don't like the kind of moral high ground it forces you to stand on.'

'Ketaki?'

'It's that position of moral superiority, you know?'

'I agree,' Adil says. 'I have a lot of trouble with forgiveness too.'

'Yes, lots of trouble,' she says.

'I prefer reconciliation. It's a lot harder, I think, but it lets you be on equal terms.'

'Reconciliation,' she repeats.

'Ketaki, why don't you sit down?' Adil holds the stool steady for her as she gets onto it again. 'Are you okay?' he says.

'I'm fine.'

'Of course, the other problem with forgiveness is the forgetting part of it,' Adil says. 'To forgive someone is to forget the hurt they committed against us – and only that, right?'

'Yes.'

'We've got to separate the action that hurt us from the perpetrator of that action, and then only forget that action.'

'Yes,' she says again.

'And that's difficult – at least that's how it first was for me with my father. I couldn't make the separation. And so what did I do? For the first couple of years after he died I just blocked him out altogether.'

'Like what my dad did with my mum.'

'Probably,' Adil says softly, head bowed, as if he were apologizing for her father.

'Maybe like what I did with my mum for all these years.'

'Yes.'

'But you were saying, about your father… '

'I was just saying that I blocked him out,' Adil says. 'So, yes, I didn't feel any resentment, but I also obliterated him from my life. Some time later, though, I realized that I needed him. Even if only as a presence, even just as memories, I needed him around. But I could only build that presence through some kind of reconciliation with him. And that's what I've been trying to do.'

'That's good.'

'Of course, I still haven't managed to work things out with my brother.'

'Maybe it's easier to work things out with dead people,' she says.

He laughs.

'But you should probably still try to talk to him. He is your brother.'

'Yes, I should.'

'Will you?'

'I plan to next month when he visits.'

'I'm going to hold you to it,' she says.

'Okay.'

'Good.'

'But all that aside for a moment, is that what you want to do with your mother? Wipe her out?'

'I had blocked her out already,' she says, taking the crumpled paper ball that was her drawing and shifting it from hand to hand. 'Before my dad told me about my mum and Deepak Uncle I only thought of her now and then. Without feeling – without longing. Maybe I knew something was up even before I was told about it and that's why I saw her only as a picture, not as a person.'

Adil wheels his chair forward towards her and rests his hands on her knees, his eyes on her eyes. She looks at him, and little by little she can feel the tension in her neck ease, the palpitation slow, her toes uncurl. 'Thank you for coming over,' she says.

He smiles. 'You're welcome,' he says.

'But honestly, I've had enough,' she says. 'I'm tired. I want her out of my head. I want her out of my life.'

'I'm pretty certain you don't want to do that,' he says. 'And if you try to work through the issues, then she could continue to live with you, and so could your uncle.'

In death, as in life, she thinks. The two of them together forever through her. 'Maybe I don't want that,' she says, her leg beginning to shake rapidly.

'Maybe you do,' Adil says, trying to hold her leg still. 'Why am I sitting here in your studio for the first time in the three years I've known you?'

'What do you mean?'

'Why have you asked me over?'

'I wanted to see you,' she says.

'Yes, but why?' he says. 'You're struggling to come to some sort of reconciliation and you need a sounding board.'

'But what if I can't?' she says.

'Then, of course, you're fucked.'

She laughs.

'But seriously, you've got to give it a try,' Adil says. 'It's hellish hard – ask me – but it's the only way.'

She inspects her thumb and pulls at a cuticle come loose on her nail.

'Ketaki?' he says, bringing her hand down.

'Yes?' she says.

'You say your uncle tried to shape you into your mother, right?'

'My aunt said that.'

'So your aunt said that and you see some truth in it?'

'Yes, I think I do,' Ketaki says. 'I mean, now when I think about it, why did he do all those things?'

'What things?' Adil says, trying to keep her seated as she tries to get up again. 'What things are you talking about?'

'Why did he spend so much time with me? Why did he push me to play tennis when I was a kid? Why the birdwatching? Why this, this studio?'

'Maybe he loved you?' Adil says.

'Then why these things in particular? Why only what my mum did?' She picks up her sketchpad from the floor and doodles aimlessly on its cover. 'But then I let him, didn't I? He couldn't have done this to me, he couldn't have manipulated me, if I hadn't let him.'

'Why do you think you let him?'

Ketaki puts down her pad and looks at Adil.

Adil looks back at her.

'I don't know,' she says. 'Why did I let him?'

'Maybe you loved him?' Adil says.

Ketaki resumes her doodling, drawing long interlocking squiggles across the cover of the sketchpad.

'I didn't know him,' Adil says, 'but I don't think he consciously sought to shape you into your mother – and neither did you consciously allow him to do so.'

'So then I should be all right with it?' she says, peering up from her pad.

'We blunder in all sorts of ways,' Adil says, 'especially in times of crisis. And we cause a lot of hurt, mostly unknowingly – and mostly towards those we love. Which is not to say that it's okay. We just need to be more aware of what we do – more aware of the consequences of what we do.'

For several minutes she stares at her doodle, then she sets the pad down on the drawing board and the charcoal stick on the pad, and turns to Adil. 'Maybe it was simply this,' she says. 'Maybe he wanted my mother and I wanted my mother and each of us found her in the other. Maybe we were just using each other.'

'Maybe,' Adil says, 'and maybe we can't always tell the difference between using and loving.'

In an instant she is off the stool and in front of him, her mouth on his, her tongue trying to drive its way through his lips. But with comparable speed and force, Adil takes hold of her by the shoulders and pushes her away from him.

'Sleeping with me won't make you feel better,' he says.

Her hand reaches for the stool to steady herself. She looks up at him, turns away, and walks over to her desk.

Adil comes up to her. 'I'm going to go now,' he whispers into her ear as she sits down. 'Call me when you want to talk.'

She senses the press of his palm on her back and then, before she knows it, it is gone.

It is hot as day at midnight when she steps out of her flat. The street is asleep; Mr Chatterji is likely asleep. Just short of a minute later she is in front of her aunt's house, viewing the last remaining single-storey bungalow in the block. She carefully unlocks the ring latch on the gate, walks around the car, and lets herself into the house through the kitchen.

Through the crack in Neera's bedroom door, the light from the bedside lamp and the air conditioner's loud song find their way into the hall. Her aunt must be awake. Ketaki moves past quickly towards the guest bedroom. Here too, the door is shut; here too, the lights are on. Ketaki steps back, stops, steps forward, then reaches for the doorknob, slowly turns it, and opens the door. Sitting erect on the hospital bed is Neera, whose sudden stiffness slackens when she recognizes the face of the intruder.

Ketaki stands at the door. 'It's hot in here,' she says. 'Can I put the fan on?'

'Yes, of course,' her aunt says, shifting to the left side of the bed.

She switches on the fan.

'It's a bit of a squeeze, but come,' Neera says, patting the empty space next to her on the mattress.

Ketaki gets into bed, the entire length of her body touching her aunt's.

'You couldn't sleep?' Neera says, twirling and twisting her Belgian lace hanky with her fingers.

'No,' Ketaki says.

'Me too.'

The room is just as it was six weeks ago, when Deepak still lived here. The hospital bed has yet to be returned, the tea trolley has not been wheeled back into the dining room, the sofa-set stays pushed against the wall by the window; everything remains in its place as if Deepak were still around. Ketaki closes her eyes, and before she quite realizes it, warm rills of tears are moving down the sides of her face. Soon her skin begins to tingle from the salt of her weeping.

Neera gives her a light kiss on the forehead. 'Let's go back to my room,' she says. 'You're right, it's very hot in here.'

Ketaki nods. Turning away from her aunt, she rubs her eyes against her sleeve and gets off the bed.

They walk through the dark hall. 'Thank god for air conditioners,' Neera says, as they enter her bedroom.

'Yes,' Ketaki says.

'Are you hungry?'

'No.'

Her aunt picks up a folder and a pile of magazines stacked in the middle of the bed, and puts them on the bedside table. From her cupboard she takes out a kurta and hands it to Ketaki.

'What?' Ketaki says.

'You should change and get into bed,' Neera says.

'Okay.' Sitting at the edge of the bed, Ketaki pulls off her jeans. She then stands up and takes off her T-shirt and her bra.

'You're losing weight,' Neera says, watching her undress. 'You're not eating properly.'

Once she has changed, Ketaki finger-brushes her teeth and lies down next to her aunt.

'Should I put the light off?' Neera says.

'I'm fine with it on,' she says.

Propping her pillow against the headboard, Neera sits up in bed. 'What did you do today?'

'Nothing much,' Ketaki says. 'Dropped Papa to the airport and came home.'

'You didn't come for dinner.'

'Adil came over.'

'Adil,' Neera says. 'Lovely boy. Well-brought up. You should bring him across some time.'

'Okay,' she says.

'So your father mentioned you're thinking of moving back to New York,' she says.

'He asked me to think about it.'

Neera reaches for the folder from her bedside and puts it on her lap. She opens it and takes out a folded blueprint.

'What's that?' Ketaki says.

'The plans,' her aunt says, unfolding the large sheet.

'Plans?'

'The architect's plans for Pangot.'

Ketaki turns onto her side.

Neera puts on her half-moon spectacles. 'So what have you thought?' she says.

'About what?' Ketaki says.

'New York,' Neera says, scrutinizing the blueprint.

'I don't know,' Ketaki says, pulling the quilt up to her chin. 'Maybe I'll just go for a holiday.'

'It's too cold there in the winter — but, of course, the decision is yours.'

'Yes.'

'Anyway, Sheila Seth's son, the architect, is quite a talented boy, isn't he?' Neera says, putting the drawing in front of Ketaki.

Ketaki nods.

Neera sets the drawing aside, adjusts her pillow, lies down, coughs, sits up, takes a sip of water, lies down again, and finally switches off the light.

Rolling onto her stomach, Ketaki closes her eyes and wills sleep upon herself, but with little luck. She turns onto her side again.

'Keta?' Neera whispers in the dark.

'Yes?' she says, opening her eyes.

'Are you awake?'

'Yes.'

'New York is really only good for a holiday.'

Ketaki inches towards her aunt, until her nose touches Neera's back. She closes her eyes. Before long she is coasting, and a wash of pre-sleep comes over her.

'Keta?' her aunt says again.

'Masi?'

'What do you think we should use for the cottage? Brick or stone?'